He stuck his hand in the window and snapped the cigarette at me. The sparks dug into my face and I lunged from the car.

He started circling me, keeping his hands low, grinning comtemptuously. I could hear his girl, breathing excitedly behind him.

In the dim light there was a sudden flash. I followed it—to his hand and the switchblade knife cutting an arc toward me. . . .

He was a small-town punk who made his point with a knife. And this time the police would stay out of it, especially since I was on the taking end. It was what they were looking for, a way of coaxing me to leave town so I'd never want to come back . . . or be able to.

JOHN D. MacDONALD

DEATH TRAP

FAWCETT GOLD MEDAL • NEW YORK

DEATH TRAP

Chapter 1

WHEN I READ THE SMALL ITEM in the Chicago paper and the whole world seemed to stop, I remembered that I had thought about Vicky that very morning, thought about her while I was shaving.

That in itself was not too much of a coincidence, because I had thought of her often during the three years since I had seen her. Usually she came into my mind when I was depressed—in the middle of a sleepless night, or during the sour mood of hangover. That was when I thought of Victoria Landy. Any thought of her was merely another way of calling myself a damn fool. You never forget the chances you have missed, the good things you have thrown away.

I felt a touch on my shoulder and looked up from the paper and realized that the waitress had been asking me something and had finally reached across the counter. "Something wrong with you?" she asked. She was blond and heavy and she looked concerned about me.

"No. I'm okay. Sorry."

"I asked if you want some more coffee."

"Yes. Thanks."

It was just a small item on a back page. I had

nearly missed it. The name had jumped out at me. Landy.

APPEAL DENIED IN LANDY CASE

Warrentown [UP]. Sept. 12. Today one of the last chances for Alister Landy, college student convicted of rape murder, flickered out when his attorney's motion for a new trial was denied. In view of the wide interest shown in the trial and the nature of the crime, informed sources say that commutation of the sentence by the Governor is highly unlikely. It is expected that a new date for the execution will soon be set.

That was all. But it was enough. It could not be a case of identical names. I could fill in too many blanks. Alister Landy had been in Sheridan College in the town of Dalton. Warrentown was the county seat, thirty-five miles away. And Alister was Vicky's kid brother.

I left the hotel coffee shop and went up to my room. I had not unwrapped some of the fishing tackle that had been delivered the day before. I unwrapped it and sat on the edge of the bed and tried to take some satisfaction from the look and feel of the good star drag reel, the fiberglass boat rod. But I couldn't stop thinking about Vicky and about what this would be doing to her.

I had thought about Vicky that same morning. I had felt depressed, and yet there were no good reasons for feeling depressed. I had just gotten back after spending two and a half years out of the country as assistant superintendent on the construction of two military airfields in Spain. Telboht Brothers, the construction firm I work for, had been the successful bidders. The job was over. I'd had enough of red tough rock and red baked sand and green local labor and broken-down equipment. I flew into Chicago and delivered some inspection reports and certifications to the home office and got straightened away with the payroll people and with the bank where my savings had been adding up.

Sitterson, the Project Superintendent, was in, and I had a talk with him. It didn't come out the way I thought it would. He seemed reserved, cool. He didn't give me any information. I finally had to ask for it.

"I'd like to take my full sixty days, Mr. Sitterson. But can you give me any idea of what job I'll be going on when I report back in?"

"Not right now. But there'll be a place for you. You know that, MacReedy."

It wasn't enough. I had expected to hear him say that they'd make me super on one of the small jobs. God knows I'd worked hard enough as Mooney's right hand man during the two and a half years in Spain. I knew every phase of the work. Maybe theory was a little shaky, but I knew all the practical angles. But Sitterson wasn't as cordial as he had been when he had flown over to check the job eight months before. He had called me Hugh then, and he had half promised a better job when the Spanish job was finished.

I couldn't figure out what had changed. Mooney had flown back to Chicago for a conference about two months ago. Probably they had discussed me.

But I couldn't see Mooney sticking a knife in me. He was too big a man to do it out of jealousy. And I knew he liked me. He was always after me to change my personal life. "Save your money, Hugh. You don't have to spend every last dime."

"It's adding up in the bank, isn't it?"

"Sure. For a big fling as soon as you get the chance. You've got a decent education, kid. You don't have to live like a construction bum."

"My father was a construction bum, Al."

"I know, I know. And you know I was a kid engineer on that Oregon bridge job when the hoist cable let go. I knew Bucky and for a little guy he was all man. And he left you and your mother without dime one."

"I've got nobody to support, Al."

"Maybe you should have."

He kept after me like that. And he didn't like it when I took ten days off in Spain. He didn't begrudge me the ten days. I had earned them. But it pained him that I should take off with Felizia and spend the ten days at Fuengirola, swimming, eating, drinking and making love instead of going perhaps to Madrid and making like a tourist.

Mooney certainly would have had to tell Sitterson that I performed on the job. If I could do the job, Telboht Brothers would make money and hit completion dates and keep the bonding companies happy. What I did in my off time was my own business.

I spent two days and nights in Chicago with friends from the home offices. I got respectably drunk, bought a car and equipment for the trip I planned. I picked the car off a lot, a two-year-old

Chrysler wagon. I found a garage that would let me use tools. I pulled the head and the wheels and found it worth buying. I installed rings, new front shocks and a new fuel pump.

Then I was ready to go. I had sixty days and it was October and I knew just what I wanted to do. I wanted to drive down to Guaymas on the Golfo de California and fish. And I didn't want to go alone. So first I would go to New Orleans and look up Scotty. Unless he had married, which was unlikely, his list would be as active as ever. And he would know what I wanted. Not a model, no young girl with delusions of eternal love—rather, a mature and restless woman who would like the idea of going with me to Mexico, who would want some laughs, want to catch some fish, and be willing to part when it was over without remorse or recriminations.

Yet on the morning of the day I planned to leave Chicago I did not feel that special sense of excitement that goes with vacation. I had sixty days and six thousand bucks to spend and a good plan for spending it, but there was no lift. Instead, there was a feeling of depression, of let-down. I tried to attribute it to hangover.

When you are depressed, the face in the mirror does not seem to be your own. My face showed a mixed heritage. My father was Scotch-Irish, a small wiry cat-quick man, tough and pugnacious, his face fist-marked by bigger men he had fought. My mother was tiny, a Pole with pale hair and tilted sea-gray eyes. Her half-dozen brothers were huge slow lumbering men. I had her eyes and her heavy Slavic cheekbones. I had his copper hair, streak-bleached by the savage Spanish sun. I had inherited height and bulk from the male side of her line, along with my father's quickness. This combination had kept me from being marked as he had been marked. A small scar here under the eye. A slight flatness at the bridge of the nose. Nothing else. The deep tan was occupational and unmistakable, a tan shared by tropical sailors, by Miami beachboys, by Colorado prospectors and by construction workers.

I shaved away stubble that was like fine copper wire. My head pulsed with the dull ache of hangover. And I thought of Vicky. I thought of what-might-have-been.

I had been an engineer on nine miles of new state highway on the Warrentown-Dalton road. We were straightening it and four-laning it. There were three big cuts, and a lot of fill. It was rolling, beautiful country. Because the job was closer to Dalton than to Warrentown, we set up just outside of Dalton. I had been there for a few days when we made the estimates for the bid, running soil tests and analyzing cores. I was in the first group to go back when our bid was the one accepted, and I worked with the boys rechecking the survey and the specifications.

Dalton was a college town. Sheridan College, a small all-male liberal arts college of good reputation. The Department of Archeology there had found some Indian relics in one of the hills where we had to make a cut. They had written to the state capital and somebody there got in touch with the home offices in Chicago and we got word in the field to co-operate with the college.

I was elected to go talk to them and find out what they wanted us to do. Sheridan College was on a hill south of the village. It was a beautiful September morning a little more than three years ago. I had rented a room in an old house just off the central square. The central square had a New England look, with big elms, walks, benches, a beat-up bandstand. There were white churches and stores and a big inn. I went back to my room and changed from sweaty khakis to slacks and a sports shirt, and drove one of the company sedans south on College Street and up the hill to the college buildings. I got there at eleven and classes were changing. College kids were criss-crossing the campus. I felt elderly and superior to them. I'd been out four years. I was twenty-six. I'd worked in Peru and in Cuba. I had been bitten by a tropical snake. I had seen a man pulled into the gearing of a stone crusher. I'd seen a gas truck slip off a mountain at dusk and, two hundred feet down the stone slope, strike and bloom like a strange blue and yellow flower. I felt superior to these kids, and slightly appalled that they should look so young.

I located the administration building and went in and found an open door. I walked in and saw a dark head bent over a list of names, saw that dark head lift and found myself looking into the blue blue eyes of Victoria Landy. Psychologists deride the concept of love at first sight as being a delusion and a rationalization of the immature. All I know is that we looked at each other for what seemed a very long time. Afterward she told me that she felt oddly breathless and slightly dizzy. That was exactly the way I felt.

I remember that I found out who I was supposed to see and she told me how to find him. I went and talked to him and he marked on my map the area he was interested in and I promised to inform him in advance of when we would start moving earth so he could put some people in his department on the scene.

Then I went back and found the dark-haired girl, and that night we had dinner together at the MacClelland Inn, on a screened side porch where the night wind ruffled the candle flames and stirred her hair.

I learned about her. She was twenty-three. She had been born and raised in Philadelphia. Her father had been an associate professor at the University of Pennsylvania. Her mother had been Italian. Her brother, the only other child, was six years younger and had just entered Sheridan College on a full scholarship. Vicky had gone to the University of Pennsylvania and, in order to help her father with the textbooks he wrote, had learned typing and shorthand. Right after her twenty-first birthday her father became eligible for a sabbatical year. Since Vicky would graduate soon and had a job promised her, and Alister was in an experimental school in Philadelphia with enrollment limited to children with an exceptionally high I.Q., she stayed to maintain the house and take care of Alister while their parents went to Italy.

They received a letter a week from them. And then Vicky received a phone call from Washington, from the State Department, informing her that Dr. and Mrs. Christopher Landy had died in a hospital in Bergamo of food poisoning. She found out later that it had been a botulism acquired from spoiled sausage, resulting in the traditional blindness, destruction of the nervous system and death. The day after notification their last letter was received, stating that they planned to visit the village where her mother's parents had been born and look up any relatives that might remain there.

She explained to me that Alister was not the sort of boy you could send off to college on his own. I could not understand that until I met him. In the experimental school he had done a paper on a proposed mathematical approach to sociology. It was that paper which had won him the Sheridan scholarship.

The people at Sheridan, after interviewing Alister, understood why her presence would be desirable for at least a year or two, and arranged to give her a job in the administrative office. She had been at work a week when I met her. Alister was living in a dormitory. She was living in a rented room in one of the faculty houses.

I do not know how to describe her. She was not at all like the women who had previously attracted me. I had preferred laughing women whose diction did not make me uncomfortable, big extroverted girls with simple hungers easily gratified—like the singer at Varadero Beach, and the Russian in Quito, and the coeds of Southern Cal where I had paid for my groceries by being a fast wingback and a long ball outfielder.

She was not tall. There was a quietness about her. She had many silences, and some of them were most solemn. Her face was so lean and controlled as to be almost ascetical, but the primness was denied by the ripeblooming flower of her mouth. Her hair was so very dark and her eyes were so very blue. She walked and moved lithely; and somehow, in the controlled sway of her small hips, there was more earthy promise than in the strut of any stripper. She looked fragile, yet on the Sunday I took her out and we walked miles on the road job, I could not tire her. In her dark conservative dresses, in the sheaths she liked to wear, you could imagine that naked she might look like a plucked bird, with lattice of ribs, immature breasts, hollow belly, concave thighs. Yet on one of the last warm days of the year I took her to a lake where we swam. Her suit was powder blue. Her arms and legs were long and round, creamy and flawless. Her breasts were deep and her hips had a rounded ripeness, almost an abundance. She swam with the easy tireless grace of an otter, and on that rare day she laughed aloud often, the laughter astonishingly deep in her throat, white teeth gleaming, black hair pasted flat on the contour of the fragile skull.

Because she was so unlike any girl I had ever known, I was not at ease with her. I moved cautiously. There was a challenge in the quality of her mind, and to meet it I did not drink heavily when we went out together. I felt no need to, and suspected that had I done so she would have shown not contempt but boredom.

We argued about her brother, about this feeling

of dedication she seemed to have. She said that he was a responsibility emotionally, yet his mind was worth any dedication. I met him. He was a misfit. He was petty, arrogant, supercilious, querulous and painfully shy. Alister was a very handsome boy. He irritated me. He was condescending to his sister, contemptuous of the school, the instructors, the other students. He could be morose, humorless and stubborn as a mule. He seemed to invite physical attack.

And yet . . . some of the things he said, the views he held . . .

Look at it this way. In my terms. Triangulation is the simplest process in civil engineering. Line up point A from points B and C and soon you know a hell of a lot more about the location of point A. Now assume that point A is, instead of a physical point, an idea. By inheritance and training and quality of mind, you are forever condemned to regard idea A from point B. You can see it in only one way. And then along comes an Alister Landy who can stand at point C and look at the same idea. It is only genius which is capable of the unique viewpoint. And the observations of genius give us our chance of seeing old ideas in new depth. This can stretch your mind, and it is a frightening thing.

Afterwards I talked to Vicky about him.

"Now you do see what I mean, Hugh."

"I think so. But he's a monster. Forgive me for saying that."

"I want you to be frank. But you're wrong. You see all the defenses. They irritate me, but not as much as they do you, because I can see underneath. I can see the frightened boy. He's almost alone in the world. He's never been able to gain social acceptance or approval. When he was little he fought hard for that approval, playing games that bored him, fighting other little boys even though he thought it was childish. But he always said the wrong thing and they set him apart and finally he decided to stay apart from them—and from all of us. He wants so desperately to be loved that he goes at it in all the wrong ways. I sensed he wanted your approval. He's a rebel, a barbarian. Already he is thoroughly disliked by the student body and most of the faculty."

"But can't they see that he's really got something special?"

She smiled slowly and the smile turned into a grin, wrinkling an ivory nose. "Now who is defending him?"

She was what I had.

It didn't take long to ruin it.

Not when my basic and instinctive reaction to the female was to attempt to rack up a score, add a pelt to the trophy shelf. I sensed it wouldn't be easy. So I went at it very carefully. And without conscience. Why should I have felt any twinge of conscience? She was of age. She was willing to go out with me. So she was taking her own chances. Plenty of others had taken their chances too, and, to the gratification of my male ego, most of them had lost the game. I didn't want to have to classify Vicky as one of the ones who got away. So I moved very carefully.

There are rules. Some people don't follow them. When you don't follow the rules, you can't rack up a legitimate score. You've cheated. The rules say that you cannot promise marriage, hint at an engagement, or even use the word love.

When I first kissed her I anticipated a tepid response, a response which would be another implied obstacle in the way. But from way back, from the groves and hillsides and yellow sun of her mother's people, came a response that was sudden and vivid and alive, like the tart-sweet taste of a good red wine. Her arms were tight and then convulsively tight, and her mouth was something soft and broken. Then she flung herself aside, moving away from me. The moon slanted down through the car window on her side, shining into her lap where her lean hands kept twisting and knotting, pulling at each other. I heard the deepness of her breathing, saw the flower-heaviness of her head, her half-closed long-lashed eyes. I knew that it would be easy then, and I was pleased and excited.

Why not? I was a construction bum. There were girls in every land. This was more special than most, but that merely made her a more desirable target. She was of age. She took her chances. And nobody had said anything about love.

I spoiled it. I worked entrapment. I moved cautiously. I betrayed her with her own deep sensuality, and at the end I closed my ears to her protests, to her fright, to her pleading. My answer was not in her voice, but in the physical indications of a passion she could not quell without my help. I did not help her.

It ended three weeks after the first kiss. It ended at midnight in a shabby room in a shabby motel on the far side of Warrentown. I lay in the darkness and smoked a cigarette. She was crying almost soundlessly beside me. I felt uneasy and uncomfortable. It was not the way it should have been.

"Why are you crying?"

She did not answer me. After what seemed a long time she stopped crying. I felt the bed move as she got up. I heard the rustle of her clothing.

"Now what are you doing?"

She turned on the light. She was dressed. I squinted into the light and pulled a corner of the sheet across myself. She looked down at me, and there were shadows under her blue eyes.

She looked down at me for a long time and then tried to smile and said, "I love you."

It was on the edge of my tongue to say the same to her, but that was not in the rule book. I guess I smiled uneasily.

"Will we be married?" she asked. It was a question so Victorian that I tried to laugh.

"Is it funny?"

"Vicky, honey, you don't understand the kind of business I'm in. Hell, next month I could be sent to Spanish Morocco."

"That isn't what I mean."

Her eyes made me feel guilty. You cover guilt with spurious anger. "No," I said. "We won't be married. Does that answer your question, darling?"

Her face was very still. She folded her arms, hugging her breasts as though she were cold. "I hope you're very proud," she said softly. "Maybe you keep a diary. Be sure to list my every reaction before you forget."

"Wait a minute, honey."

"Could you please get dressed? I'll wait in the car."

She had nothing to say on the way back. I do not mean that she made evasive answers. She would not open her mouth. After I got back to my place I could not get to sleep. I felt uncomfortable, and did not know why. After all, I had scored. Mission accomplished. She would get over being haughty. I told myself that I felt uneasy because she had been a virgin. I had not expected that and had, in fact, come very close to ending it when I found out. But in the dark room, in the dark bed, next to warmth and shivering eagerness tempered by fright, that brand of will power is an unusual commodity indeed.

She would come around, I told myself. I would have to apologize, get a chance to talk to her. It would be all right.

But I never heard another word from her lips, except when she would answer the phone. As soon as she recognized my voice there would be a soft decisive click and a dead line. I waited for her. I walked with her. I tried to talk to her. She walked with a lithe, even stride, never glancing at me or speaking. I could have been an invisible, inaudible man. She became visibly thinner and more pale. I wrote to her. There was no answer. I was certain she did not open the letters. I was still trying when I was transferred to the Spanish airfield job. And by then I knew what I had lost, what I had spoiled. Realization was a long time in coming; and when it came in all its intensity, I knew that the world seldom saw as great a fool as I. She had magic, integrity, passion and a rare loveliness. And I had gone at her the way you go at one of those coin machines where you try to pick up the prize with a toy crane. I could have had the whole machine, with all the prizes and all the candy. But I had settled for gilt and glass.

Other girls became tasteless. The gusto had gone out of the game. One breast was too like another; hips could move in identical cadence.

Time did not seem to soften the sense of loss. Had I come back from Spain sooner, I would have tried to see her. But I knew it would be the same; so I stayed away, forgoing my chances of quick trips back to the States until the sense of loss was dulled, until there were days and weeks when I could forget her entirely. Yet on the sour mornings, or during the nights I could not sleep . . .

And this morning there was no need for depression. I forced Vicky out of my mind by thinking about Scotty, wondering about what he could provide. In Guaymas I would rent a cruiser after I learned the waters. Maybe about twenty-six foot, with good bunks, a decent galley. Anchor for the night. Go over the side in first light, down into the gray warm water.

Then I went down to breakfast and found the clipping and went back up to the room. It was Alister Landy, her brother. I had met him; yet I could not say if it was possible or impossible for him to commit rape and murder.

It was all over now. The kid would be electrocuted. He would be nineteen now, or perhaps twenty. She would be twenty-six. And in five months I would be thirty. Perhaps she has married. She would not care to see me. There is too much on her mind. There is nothing I can do. Drive on down and see Scotty. Ignore it. Forget her. Don't go near her. It will just make the pain sharp again and there is nothing in all the world you can do to mend what you spoiled.

Chapter 2

I KEPT CHECKING THE MAP as I drove south. And I knew when I came to the crossroads. I could turn east at that junction, toward Dalton. Or continue south. I arrived at the crossroads at three o'clock on the thirteenth of October, on Thursday afternoon. There was a big truck stop. I pulled in and parked. I sat at the counter and had coffee. I could see the phone booth in the back. I kept turning and looking at it.

Finally I stood up slowly, wearily. I went to the cashier and got change. I shut myself into the booth and dialed long distance. She gave me the college. A woman answered. I put the coins in the box.

"I'd like to speak to Miss Landy, please. Miss Victoria Landy."

The woman hesitated and said, "She is no longer employed here."

"Would you know where I can reach her?"

She asked me to hold the line. She came back on and gave me a phone number in the village. I thanked her and got the operator and gave her the number and made the call person-to-person. I had about a half minute wait.

"I'm sorry, but that number has been disconnected."

I thanked her and went back to the counter and had more coffee. I thought of her pride, and her gentleness, and the way she would lift her blue eyes to mine as the slow smile came. I paid for the coffee and picked up some cigarettes and walked slowly out to the wagon. I got in and sat for a long time before I started it up and headed east, driving too fast.

It was late when I drove into Warrentown. I passed the motel where it had ended. A lighted sign said, *Under New Management.* I stayed at a newer place down the road. After I checked in, I drove into town. Warrentown is a small city of about thirty thousand. I found a bar. I could be thirty-five miles from Vicky. Or if she had gone up to stay near the prison, she could be a hundred miles away. I knew I would find her tomorrow. It made me feel empty in the middle. And lost.

The bar was crowded. It was a neighborhood place. I found room at the curve of the bar. They stare at you in a neighborhood place and try to figure you out. It makes a short hush in the conversation and then they go on as before. A husband and wife team near me were having a deadly almost inaudible quarrel. She was drunk, her face loose, her eyes glittering, her fist opening and closing in a puddle of beer. They left soon, her face mirroring the pain of his hard hand on her arm. It gave me room to expand a little. I looked around without being too obvious about it, and picked my pigeon. He was a little guy, about fifty, well-dressed, with quick shrewd eyes. When I had a chance I moved next to him.

When he glanced at me I said, "Is this the town where they had the trial of the Landy kid?"

"Just passing through?"

"Stopping in a motel down the road."

"This is where we held the circus, friend. And where were you? I thought every literate person in this great nation knew the fame of Warrentown. And most of the illiterates."

"I was in Spain. I only heard about it the other day. Construction work."

"I've got a son-in-law in that game, friend. Right now he's in Panama."

I didn't want the conversation to get away from me. "I guess people got pretty excited about the Landy case."

The man nodded. "He damn near didn't come to trial. They got their timing right for once and sent a guard detachment in here. I guess you read about that."

"I don't know anything at all about it. I don't know who he killed or where he killed her or anything about it."

"He was a weird boy, mister. I guess I can use his name in the past tense without being too inaccurate. Too many brains. Like that Loeb and Leopold team years ago. I guess he figured that the laws of decency that apply to you and me didn't apply to him. He was going to college over there in Dalton. Sheridan College. He was in his last year. He was running around with an eighteen-year-old girl named Nancy Paulson. She had a kid sister named Jane Ann Paulson, age sixteen. It just so happens that I know Dick Paulson, the father. Now I'm not the sort of guy to claim we were bosom buddies. But I did meet him a couple of times when I was over in Dalton on business. Dick owns a market over there. Good meats. He gets a high-class trade. This Landy boy had the use of a car. It was his sister's car. She was working for the college at that time. You understand, this all happened way back in April, six months ago.

"Anyway, all of a sudden Jane Ann Paulson is missing. She'd been in some kind of Christmas pageant so there was a real good picture of her. Pretty little kid. It really stirred up the area. They had everybody and his brother out hunting for her, and cops from all over, and everybody trying to get in on the act. She turned up missing on a Friday night, I think it was. She had a girl friend in her class in high school, daughter of one of the professors lived up on the hill. The last anybody saw of Jane Ann, she was walking up the hill. But she never got there. Some farm kid found the body the following Wednesday afternoon in an aspen patch near Three Sisters Creek. She was naked and dead, raped and cut up some.

"Then the fun really started. The college boys park with their dates on a side road near where the body was found. Feeling ran pretty high in Dalton. There wasn't a college boy who would have dared go down into the village alone. A smart state cop took over. He figured that the kid had to have been taken out there by car. It was five miles beyond the college, and over six miles from the village. He impounded every car that college kids had the use of. While the other police were rounding up known sex deviates, the state cop had lab tests run on a hundred and twelve automobiles. It took time. But they came up with the right car. It was the Ford that belonged to Landy's sister. Blood had been scrubbed off the upholstery, but they took the fabric off and they got enough from the underside to run off the type. It matched the kid's blood.

"That cop, Frank Leader his name is, was too smart to jump quick. He wanted to sew it up good; and he did. The Landy boy lived with his sister in a small apartment in an old house in the village. Leader found cleaning fluid there that he could tell—or the lab could tell—had been used on the car seat. And he found the rag and the lab was able to show it was human blood on the rag, even though they couldn't type it. They'd vacuumed the car out and got female hair and did comparisons and found two of the hairs were from the dead girl's head. Leader wanted the knife and he wanted to find the pocketbook the girl had been carrying. They really tore up that place. Found the pocketbook and the knife buried in a flower bed in the yard. It was a new knife, a paring knife. Leader traced it to a hardware store in Dalton. He was able to prove Landy had been in the store a few days before the murder. Nobody sold him a knife, but they were on open display."

"Did he confess?" I asked.

"No. With all they had stacked up against him, he might just as well have. The ground was soft at that lover's lane place. A smart speed cop kept people off the parking places until he could get help. They took molds of the tire tracks and matched one up with the Ford."

"What was the defense?"

"The old yelp—you know—it's all circumstantial. Landy had no alibi for the time. April the sixth, I think it was. Anyway, it was a Friday. His sister had a date. She'd come over here by bus in the middle of the afternoon to do some shopping and the guy she was dating met her over here for dinner. She didn't take the car because it was in the repair garage. Landy got it out of the garage at five. The service manager said the kid acted funny. He drove back to the apartment. The prosecution proved the car was there at five-fifteen and gone by five-thirty. He was in the habit of going and taking rides all by himself. His sister testified to that. He was a funny-acting kid. No friends. He said he got back to the house about nine. His sister said he was asleep when she got back. He didn't have a date with Nancy Paulson because they'd had some sort of a scrap that week." He looked at his watch. "Hell, I've got to be rolling, fellow. You should have seen this town when the trial was going on. All the wire services and television and hundreds of newspaper guys and cranks from all over. That little town and the college won't recover for a long time."

He paid his bar check and as he started to leave, I said, "Is the sister still around?"

"I suppose so. I don't know."

I drove over to Dalton the next morning. It was a beautiful fall morning. The leaves of the big trees in the square were changing. The town had changed very little. The Dalton National Bank had had a face-lifting. Some of the stores had new plastic fronts. A Friday, the fourteenth of October. The same pre-school kids were fumbling around with the same soggy football in the park. Two young housewives walked diagonally across the park, talking as they pushed the carriages, groceries piled in beside the kids. There was a new traffic light where College Street came out onto the square. The red bus to Warrentown was waiting in the same place as before.

I parked, locked the wagon, and walked slowly in the sunlight and I *knew* she was in the town. I knew she was close. And I wanted to turn and run. I was ashamed of what I was—or what I had been.

I was wondering who to ask when I thought of a very simple solution. The phone had been disconnected but it was probably still listed. And it was. Landy, Victoria, 28 Maple. I knew Maple ran into the square at the north. I walked. Number twenty-eight was a block and a half down Maple, on the left. It was a big, elderly frame house painted an ugly reddish brown. There was a shallow porch around two sides, an ornate cupola, stained glass windows on either side of the front door, a waist-high iron fence.

An old lady was raking leaves in the yard. She wore a blue and white print dress and a man's green cardigan sweater much too big for her. When I turned in at the walk she stopped raking and watched me as I walked up to her. She had hard little eyes and a mean little mouth.

"Yes?"

"I'm looking for a Miss Landy."

"Around at the side, but she won't talk to any newspaper or magazine people. Don't cut across my lawn. You go on out to the sidewalk and back in that other gate over there. She's packing and she'll be gone by Monday and let me tell you there won't be anybody in this neighborhood or this whole town that won't be glad to see the last of anybody around here with the name Landy. I wanted to get her out of my house before, but Jud Cowan told me so long as she paid her rent I didn't have any way of getting rid of her. It seems like a very strange law to me that says a decent woman has to put up with having the sister of a murderer living in her very own house and not be able to do anything about it."

The shrill whining voice followed me until I was around the corner of the house and out of sight. Though the front yard was narrow, the grounds behind the house seemed extensive. A small conservatory bulged from the flank of the house. It was an architectural afterthought, with narrow windows and an ugly roof. The path led to two stone steps, a screen door. As I walked to the steps, feeling more tremulously uncertain than ever before in my life, I could see movement through the glass. I stood and looked through the screen. Morning light through all the windows illuminated the room.

Vicky was there. There were open cartons on the floor. She was emptying bookshelves. She wore gray slacks, a man's white shirt with the sleeves rolled up. Her dark hair was tied back. Her waist looked very narrow, her arms thin. She seemed to move with a stubborn weariness as she knelt and put the books neatly in the open carton. There was a smudge of dust on her cheek, other dust marks on the front of the white shirt. Her face was of an ivory pallor, lightly touched by the sun of the summer just past. Her facial bones seemed sharp against her skin.

She must have seen me, a tall shadow, out of the corner of her eye. She looked up quickly, half-flinching as she did so, in the manner of a small animal beaten too often. That reflex pinched my heart. She recognized me and she came very slowly to her feet, her eyes going wide. I tried to say her name but my mouth was too dry. The wide blue eyes closed and she put her hand to her throat. She tottered and I pushed the screen door open and went in and caught her, my hands on her shoulders, the bones under the flesh narrow and fine under my hands.

She opened her eyes again and there was the dazed, unfocused look of someone drugged. She said my name, said, "Hugh," so softly that it was less an audible sound than a touch of warm exhalation against my throat. She let herself come forward, lean against me. I put my arm around her. The edge of my jaw touched the dark crown of her head.

"What have they done to you, Vicky?" I asked softly. "What in the world have they done to you?"

And as I looked across her shoulder, as I looked

down through one of the windows, I found myself staring into the narrow venomous face of the old lady. She stood out there with the rake, looking in at us with spite and satisfaction.

Vicky stirred in my arms and pulled herself away. I released her. Her face was cool again, and apart from me.

"I'm very sorry," she said. "I haven't been entirely well. I feel faint quite often. I'm sorry." She moved away from me, putting half-packed cartons between us.

"I just heard about it, Vicky, just the other day. I was out of the country. I didn't know about it."

"I thought everybody in the world knew about it."

"You know that if I had known, I would have come sooner." And I tasted the shape of the lie on my mouth. I had nearly gone by. I had nearly gone on south because of fear and shame.

"Why?" The question was cool and blunt.

I made a helpless gesture with my hands. It wasn't something you could explain in one minute or one hour. "I want to help you."

"There's no way I can be helped." She went over to a narrow padded bench by the windows and sat down, took cigarettes from the shirt pocket, lighted one. There was a heavy wooden packing case already nailed up near the bench. I sat on it. I felt heavy and awkward and stupid, with hands too big and rough and brown, with feet too heavy. I looked at the floor, and then at the narrow and delicate shape of her ankles, at sandals which could not conceal the high patrician arch of her foot. I looked at her face until she looked away. There were sallow patches under her eyes, fine brackets around the contradictory mouth.

"I want to try to help."

Her voice became hard. "I do not want that kind of help. I don't care to be helped because, strange as it may seem to me, your conscience might hurt a little. It must hurt, or you wouldn't have come here. The whole thing seems odd to me."

"All right. Get out all the little whips. So it wasn't like that when I walked in here. It wasn't like that at all. Your face was different. Your voice was soft. It was all right to have me hold you."

She flushed and lifted her chin. "Don't get stupid ideas from that kind of weakness, Hugh. I'm vulnerable right now."

I hit my fist on the packing case. "Skip all that. Forget all that. Maybe it's conscience. It probably is. Is that such a bad thing? I want to help you. What are you going to do? Where are you going?"

"I—I thought I'd go up and be near him until—" She twisted her face away, then covered her face with her hands. Then came the small, lost, stifled sound of tears. I sat there awkwardly until I could stand it no longer and then I went over and sat beside her and tried to touch her on the shoulder, turn her into my arms. She moved violently away from me. Then she got up quickly, hiding her face, and left the room, going into the other part of the apartment. I stood up, knowing I could not leave. I looked around. They had apparently used the conservatory as a living-room. Out the back windows I could see two cars parked in the rear of the house, a high old Dodge, and a Chevy coupé about five years old. I heard water running. I waited for a time and then began to pack the rest of the books.

It must have been ten minutes later that she spoke, standing behind me. "Please don't do that. Please go, Hugh. I mean it."

I had been trying to think of some way to tell her. I stood up and turned and said, "I'll go. But please let me do one thing."

"No."

"It's a very simple thing. It won't cost you anything. I want you to sit over there beside me and I want to be able to hold your hand and I want to talk to you for maybe ten minutes. You don't have to say anything."

"No."

"Please, Vicky. I'm begging you. I'm asking very humbly. Please."

"All right."

She sat primly. She extended her hand to me with as much warmth as though she were reaching it out to touch nastiness. I took it in both of mine. It was cool, dry and utterly flaccid. And I did not know how to start.

"Listen," I said. "I've been in Spain. I've worked with those people. I like them. They've got pride. They've got self-respect. And a kind of passionate honesty. There was this boy, Felipe. A village boy. We taught him to drive a truck. After we started paving we put him on one of the big mixers. He was bright and quick. He took a lot of pride in how fast he could work the controls, drop the scoop and so on. When he came to work with us, he came with his best friend, Raoul. Raoul wasn't too bright. He wasn't good around equipment. He was tough and strong and willing, but he didn't fit into the machine age.

"Listen to what happened. There are guards, metal guards, where the big scoop comes down. So nobody can walk under the scoop from the side, by accident. But somebody could walk in from the front. So we have a mirror rigged. The operator is supposed to glance in the mirror before dropping the scoop. It comes down fast and hard. It weighs maybe a ton and a half. But on the job the mirror gets coated with dust, and the operator ignores it.

"Felipe was running the mixer, full of pride. Raoul walked under from the front. Felipe dropped the scoop on him. He lived for two days and then died. Felipe was with him every minute of the two days and with him when he died. The next day I caught Felipe just in time. He'd wound wire around his arm as a crude tourniquet. He had an ax from stores. He was about to take his right hand off at the wrist. The right hand was the one on the control that drops the scoop. It was an infantile reaction. It was a stupid thing to try to do. It was remorse. And grief. I stopped him."

Her hand stirred in mine. I could not look at her face. "I don't understand."

"I couldn't cut my heart out, Vicky. I couldn't go backward in time and mend things. I know there are things you can never mend. I'll just tell you this. I've been ashamed. For three years. I'm not the person I was then. I've thought of you for three years. Sometimes I've been able to forget you for as long as two weeks. But you always came back, and everything is just as vivid."

"I hope—I hope your three years have been hell."

Startled, I looked into her face. Tears stood on dark lashes and the blue eyes were hot and angry.

"But, Vicky, I—"

She snatched her hand away and jumped up, the look of weariness gone. "My three years have been hell. How many times do you think I told myself you were cruel, sly and unimaginative? That you just played a part to help you get what you wanted? That you were not worth pain, or a second thought? That you were a part of growing up, my growing up? Now you come back. I want the courage to spit on you. I—I—don't want to love you any more. I'm so dirty awful tired of loving you, Hugh."

She sagged and half fell forward into my arms, her face contorted with pain. It was a curious experience to hold her like that. She was like a transformer taking too heavy a load. She was taut, trembling so intensely it seemed more like a hum than a physical reaction. I sensed that she was on the edge of breakdown, that the world had been too much for her. I held her for a long time. Her breathing slowed and deepened. I turned her until I could see her face. It was slack, lips parted. Emotional exhaustion had pushed her over the edge and she had fallen into a deep sleep. She was limp and boneless as a doll. I left her there and walked back into the other rooms. I found her bedroom. I turned the bed down, then went back to her. I took off her sandals, then carried her in, put her in the bed, covered her lightly, and closed the door gently as I left the bedroom.

I went back out and picked up one of the sandals and studied it, and tapped it against the palm of my hand. Love makes a curious transformation in physical objects. Another woman's sandals, scuffed as these were, with worn straps, with buckle marks on the straps, would have been meaningless. But these were hers and these were dear. There could be nothing about her that was not endearing. A smudge on her cheek, a blemish on her skin, a broken bra strap, lipstick on the edge of a cup—all the things that, had they referred to someone else, would have been nothing. Love creates its own symbolism, and touches the meanest things with magic.

I do not think I had ever felt so good in my life.

I continued the packing, being very quiet. I did all I could see to do. By mid afternoon I was ravenous. I heard her call my name, faintly, tentatively. I went quickly to her. She sat on the bed.

"This is—so silly. It's like I dreamed things. But I feel all soft and weak. As if I couldn't stand up."

"You've been going on nerve too long. Don't try to get up."

She smiled and I went to her. "Is it true?" she asked.

I nodded solemnly. "All true. I love you. That's all I had to say three years ago."

"That's all you had to say, Hugh."

"And I was too stupid to say it. It was against the rules."

"What rules?"

"You wouldn't understand. It's a game I gave up. I got too old for the game."

I kissed her, and the second time I kissed her, her lips were salt. I made her stay there. I went out and made some purchases and drove the car back and fixed food for her.

After we had eaten, I said, "Now you'll let me help you."

She studied me for a long time. "There's only one way you can help me. I don't want to say this to you, but I have to. Maybe I am too emotionally involved with Al. Maybe we were too close, closer than a brother and sister should be. I want—everything for us, Hugh. But I'm not going to be any good. I can feel that. When they—kill him, part of me is going to die and never be any good to you. If he lived, I think I could in time transfer that part to you. Do you know what I mean?"

"I think I do, Vicky."

"I'm very earnest about this. Maybe the part that will die will be—how to be gay. How to laugh. You see—" She touched my hand. "—if this is a true thing now between us, Hugh, and you help me, it will be helping us."

"You've lost me."

"No matter what I feel or what you feel, I won't inflict on you the woman I will be after they—do that to him. And I mean that, with all my heart. Nothing can change my mind."

And I knew nothing could.

"So how do I help, Vicky? What do I do?"

Her thin fingers tightened on my wrist and her

eyes were direct and fierce and blue. "He didn't do it, Hugh. He didn't do it."

"But—"

"I know. I know the way it all sounds. I know the terrible sound of it. He didn't do it. And there's nothing I can do to prove he didn't. Maybe you can. I don't know. But you see—It's our only chance, the only chance we'll ever have. I won't go away, Hugh. I'll stay here, so I can help you. And—we won't have much time."

"How much?"

She whispered and she looked like a ghost. "Ten days, Hugh. They've set the date again. Ten days. They'll do it on Monday, on the twenty-fourth. In the morning."

Chapter 3

I TOOK A ROOM THAT NIGHT at the MacClelland Inn. The last thing she said to me as I left her was that she felt as though she had begun to live again. No matter how I tried to caution her, she could not stem the rising tide of her own optimism. It was a bigger responsibility than I cared to have. I knew that if I could do nothing, and I expected to be able to do nothing, the blow of his execution would be greater than if I had never come to see her. I could not endorse her faith in his innocence. I knew that whenever such a crime occurs, those close to the criminal find it impossible to believe that such a thing could be done by someone they have known and loved.

And I knew my own limitations. I was no experienced investigator. I did not know this town well, or these people. And Alister had certainly inspired no trust or affection in me. Also I anticipated that there would be a lot of feeling against anyone who tried to help him. On the other side of the ledger, I had hired and fired and managed a lot of human beings. You learn how to improve your snap judgment. You learn how you have to lean on this one and tease that one. I knew that I wasn't in any sense what could be called a timid man. And I had some money—at least enough to finance my own investigation.

I had stayed at the MacClelland Inn before for a day or two while locating a room when I had first come to the Dalton area. It was a big place and it had once been a private home. It was right on the square, a white frame place with good plantings and a comfortable colonial look about it. The furniture in the lounge was authentic antique. The rooms were large, comfortable and furnished in taste. I had eaten there many times, particularly when the brass had been in town. At that time I had gotten friendly with the owner, Charles Staubs, and his wife, Mary. I didn't know if they would remember me. He was a graduate of a good school of hotel management, a hard-working guy with sense enough to conceal the wry and somewhat cynical side of his nature from the cash customers who wouldn't appreciate it.

Mary came out to the small desk in the hallway when I rang the bell on the desk. She was a dark-haired comfortable woman. She had done the decorating, and I had suspected, three years ago, that it was Mary who kept a firm dark eye on the finances.

She glanced at me curiously. I asked for a room and she said they could give me one. I signed the register card. She looked at it and said, "Of course! How stupid! In this business I'm supposed to remember faces, aren't I? Are you building us another superhighway, Hugh?"

"Just passing through."

"I hope you've eaten. The dining-room just closed ten minutes ago."

"I've eaten. Charlie around?"

"He's in the office making out some kind of a report. State unemployment or something."

"If he isn't too tied up, I'll buy him a drink down in the Brig in about ten minutes."

"I think he'll be glad to break away."

I went up to the room and unpacked my stuff with the efficiency of a great deal of practice. My possessions are down to a severe minimum. Apart from clothing—and not too much of that—I have a thin black folder of photographs of jobs I have worked on, crews I have worked with, and a few photographs from way back. Then there are some personal papers: birth certificate, Navy discharge, diploma. And there is the revolver, a Smith and Wesson .38 in a spring clip belt holster worn shiny from wearing it on the jobs where you had to wear it, on those jobs where the junglies would come out and snatch a can of gas on the dead run.

I went on down to the basement, to the Brig. When I had been in town before it had been a favorite hangout of the kids from Sheridan College. The Staubs had acquired somewhere the crude iron door from an early American cell and incorporated it into the décor. The walls were hung with antique manacles, whips, goads and other implements of lusty pioneer punishment. There were two sets of authentic stocks. The décor was macabre, but it seemed to appeal to the college trade. Six college kids sat at one of the big trestle tables drinking beer and talking in low tones. There were two others at one of the smaller tables. I had expected to see a lot more business on a Friday night. I had a drink at the bar and in a few minutes Charlie came up beside me. We shook hands. He acted genuinely glad to see me. We took our drinks over to a far corner.

"Where's all your business, Charlie?"

He shrugged. "It'll come back, I hope. I guess you can say the village is being sort of boycotted by the kids up on the hill. Can't blame them too much. You know, in the old days there used to be a lot of trouble between the town and the college. It had all died out. Then we had the murder. Before they caught up with the Landy kid, things were rough around here. Town toughs beat up some of the hill kids, and vice versa. The college fathers declared the village off limits. Before that happened some of my more stupid fellow merchants were giving the college kids the business. Now when they get a night out, they go over to Warrentown. But they're beginning to drift back. It's hard to preserve a united front through the summer vacation. But don't think this town is going to forget quick." He shook his head sadly. Charlie is a balding man, thickening around the middle, with the bland wise eyes of the professional host.

"Everybody is pretty certain the Landy kid did it?"

He gave me a shocked look. "My God! Certain? There isn't a single shred of doubt."

"His sister doesn't think he did it."

He tilted his head to one side and looked at me quizzically. "Now I remember. I should have remembered that, Hugh. You and Vicky. And stars in her eyes. You know, I guessed wrong on that one. I never thought it would blow up. You both used to look so sold on each other."

"Maybe it's starting up again."

"It would be good for her. You ought to get her out of this town. People go out of their way to give her a bad time. There's no sense to it, but they do it. The way they act, you'd think she handed him the knife and made the suggestion. There's even dirty talk about them sharing the apartment. A boy and his sister. Imagine! Get her out of town if you can. Where have you been working?"

"Spain, ever since I left here. To get back to Vicky, I understand the college fired her."

"Fast. They never stick their neck out up there on the hill. An aristocracy of fear. That's what they've got up there. A lot of tired little feuds and jealousies and cliques. They were delighted when Frank Leader put together the airtight case against Landy. It took the heat off the school. So they helped jump on the kid. You know, big thoughtful opinions about how the kid was emotionally unstable, brilliant but erratic."

"Charlie, I think this must be about the fifth time I've ever had a chance to sit around and talk to you, but I have the feeling we know each other pretty well."

"An ominous approach, friend."

"I can ask you this. I've promised Vicky that I would dig around a little and see if I can find something that will take Alister off the hook."

"Why didn't you make some other promises too? Like gnawing down all the elms in the square with your own little teeth."

"It can't be that bad."

Charlie turned his glass slowly between thumb and forefinger. "I'll make a classic understatement, Hugh. I'll say that it was an unpopular crime around these parts. Jane Ann was a pretty kid. This is a town that goes for kids. We've got good schools, good recreation programs. There isn't much juvenile delinquency. But there are some bad apples. The kids at Sheridan are, for the most part, good kids. I'll tell you how we all feel. We feel as if we had a monster among us. We didn't know it. Now we know it can happen, and did happen, and, following the logical pattern, can happen again. There can be other monsters. Dalton isn't immune any more. We don't look at each other the same way we used to. But get this. We do feel a little comfortable that at least we got the monster isolated and out of the way. Anybody who goes around with any idea of trying to prove he didn't do it is going to be very unpopular. Because that implies that we've still got a monster running around loose. Until Frank Leader proved Landy did it, you never saw a town locked up like this one was."

"Suppose I have to try?"

"Then be just as discreet as you can be."

"Can you think of any starting place?"

"If I could think of one, the defense could have thought of one. That defense lawyer was good. John Tennant. I hear it hasn't done him much good to have taken the case. Maybe you could talk to him. It might give you some kind of a lead."

I picked Vicky up at eight o'clock on Saturday morning. The old woman glowered at us from a front window of the house. Vicky looked better. She said she had slept deeply for the first time in months. We had breakfast at a roadside place ten miles out of Dalton on the Warrentown road. It was one of a chain operation, comfortable, clean, efficient and characterless. I had not yet made a complete adjustment to having been away for two and a half years. It seemed to me that standardization had been accelerated, perhaps by television. There was less difference between the new cars, between the women, between all conversations. All seemed predigested and tasteless. I knew that in this place we could get ham and eggs that would not differ one milligram in weight or one half degree in serving heat from the same dish in the same chain a thousand miles away. It was all predictable, all designed to eliminate risk. I looked across the small table at her. She was not a part of this standardization. Her mind did not work in the flat, trite, acceptable ways. In our own way we were both aliens, nonconforming, bored with all the reassurances of a cooky-cut world.

And, with an animal egocentricity, I knew that we were looked at, speculated about. The dark and lovely girl who looked as though she were recovering from some illness. And that deeply tanned man, gray eyes pale in his face. See them talk so intently. See her bend forward, with earnest mouth and look of pleading.

"The first lawyer was from Dalton. His name is Cowan. When he found out what evidence there was, he backed out. He said it was too small a town. He named some people in Warrentown who might take it. I asked him the name of the best man. He said the best was John Tennant but he didn't think Tennant would touch it. I drove over and talked to Mr. Tennant. I called him that then. I call him John now. He became a friend. He said he would have to talk to Alister first. They had put Alister in the County Jail in Warrentown. He went down and talked to him for a long time. And then he said he would take it. I won't tell you any more. I want you to talk to him."

"Should we make an appointment?"

"Perhaps we should. I'll call from here."

She didn't have change so I gave her some. I waited at the table over a fresh cup of coffee, watched her walk away from me toward the booth. She wore a gray sweater with an intricate stitch, a gray flannel skirt, very short. Her dark hair was not lustrous as I remembered it, gleaming with health. It was dulled and lifeless. But in her walk, despite the ten pounds she had lost, there was the same unconscious, unplanned provocation.

As I settled back to wait, I overheard a snatch of

conversation from two booths away, a heavy voice.
". . . her all right. It never got in the papers. And
they didn't have to bring it up at the trial. But you
figure it out. They were living there in the apartment together. I got the cold dope. It wasn't normal, Ed. It wasn't normal at all." The voice was
oily, insinuating.

"Who's the guy with her?"

"They locked up the other one. She'd got to have
somebody. She's that type. She's the one got the
kid so heated up he went out and . . ."

I turned all the way around. The conversation
stopped. The man was in his fifties, with a loose
gray face, small avid eyes. His companion, with
his back to me, was thin and redheaded and going
bald. The man licked his lips and looked away. The
thin one turned around and stared at me.

I was about to turn back. I had myself under
control. Everything was fine. But the redhead had
to say, "Something on your mind?"

"Not a thing. Want a suggestion?"

Grayface was emboldened by his friend's antag-
onism. "Not from you, friend."

"I thought you boys might go get a good dry-
cleaning job. On the inside. A nice mental deter-
gent maybe."

The waitress hovered, obviously nervous. Redhead was the one with the guts. Or maybe he
thought all scenes of violence were limited to Saturday night taverns. He got up and came to my
table. He leaned a freckled hand on the table. He
had a wide loose mouth, a rasping voice, a florid
necktie without tie clip.

"You need a lesson in manners," he said. "And

maybe you need better taste in girl friends. That floozy you're with—"

His tone was loud. All the clink and rustle of the sounds of eating had ceased. I do not know how he planned to finish the sentence. I pushed his left hand off the table with my left hand. Simultaneously I grabbed the dangling gaudy necktie with my right hand and yanked down as hard as I could. He came down hard. His teeth clicked as his chin hit the formica table top. His eyes rolled vaguely and he sat gently on the restaurant floor. I put money on top of the check, got up and stepped across his legs. I turned and looked at Grayface. He stayed put, reaching nervously and absently for his coffee, looking everywhere but at me or his friend. The manager had appeared from somewhere. I went to the phone booth. Vicky smiled at me and hung up and came out of the booth. She saw the manager helping redhead to his feet.

"What happened?"

"Let's get out of here."

A mile down the road she said, "It was about me, wasn't it? I mean that's what started it."

"Yes. Things they said."

"Don't let it bother you, Hugh. They say things loud so I can hear. I don't let myself listen. It's filth. I know why it started. Silly reasons. Al and I were close. You know that. I guess I was the only person in the world he could be halfway normal with, affectionate with. Sometimes, when we walked, we would hold hands. It was brother-sister, and a sort of reassurance to him. Nothing else. I kissed him once in public. He had won a prize. It embarrassed him terribly. None of that would have mattered. But afterward they remembered it, and twisted it. Maybe you wonder why we moved to the apartment. He said that one year in the dormitory was all he could stand. He was never young the way the other students were young. The noise kept him from working as hard as he wanted to work. And also it was expensive, maintaining two places. And I guess—after you left—I didn't want to be alone."

"Please don't think you have to explain."

"But don't let them bother you. Try not to hear them."

"Okay. What about Tennant?"

"He wants us to come out to his house. I was there several times before."

The Tennant home was in a new exclusive housing project south of Warrentown. All roads curved. There was a new shopping section, transplanted trees of respectable size, a community playground. He was at number eight, Anchor Lane. It was compromise-modern, redwood with shed roof and a big overhang. I parked in the drive beside a little khaki Volkswagen.

"He said to come out into the backyard," Vicky told me.

We walked around the house. John Tennant was standing in an empty rectangular swimming pool. He and two small children were dressed in swimming trunks and they were painting the inside of the pool, putting fresh aqua paint over the faded paint of last year. He smiled up at us from the deep end and put the brush on the can and climbed up the ladder. He was a Lincolnesque man, brown and shambling and with deepset eyes. He had a thick thatch of undisciplined iron-gray hair. He had aqua spots on his chest but he was not as liberally daubed as the two kids.

The two kids, a boy of about ten and a girl a little older, said, "Hi," to Vicky, and, after Vicky had introduced me to John, he turned and said, "You kids keep going there. Keep up a good pace and maybe you get a bonus on the movie money."

He picked up a dirty robe from the apron of the pool and shouldered into it. "Hot enough down in there, but a little chilly out in the wind. Kind of barren labor too. The damn thing will crack again this winter and the patch job will spoil the paint job."

I looked at the pool. I could see where old cracks had been cemented. They were all within two feet of the top of the pool.

"Design it yourself?"

"And built it myself," he said. "With some neighborhood help. Maybe this time it won't crack. That paint is supposed to be more waterproof."

"It isn't water that's doing it," I told him.

"Then what is, Mr. MacReedy?"

"Your cracks are all above the frost line. Ground freezes in winter and you get some expansion there and it pushes against the pool."

"You seem to know what you're talking about. Is there any solution? Revision, please. Any cheap solution?"

The pool apron was narrow, only some eighteen inches wide. "There's one that will just take some labor. Trench all the way around it, outside the apron. Go down three feet, straight. I bet the apron has buckled during the winter too."

"Every winter."

"Trench it and use shallow forms and pour concrete, so you'll have a wider apron and empty space under the extension. Better put some reinforcing bars in the concrete. Leave the forms in. Treat the wood first. Cuprinol is good. Then you won't have enough mass pushing against your walls to crack them, and you'll have a wider apron. It's a makeshift, but it ought to work."

"Hugh is in the construction business," Vicky said.

"Home builder?" he asked.

"Highways, bridges, airfields. I met Vicky when I was working on the new piece on the Dalton-Warrentown road three years ago. I've been in Spain for the last two and a half years, Mr. Tennant. I didn't know anything about—Vicky's trouble."

We walked over to a redwood table and outdoor chairs in a corner of the yard. Tennant took cigarettes out of the pocket of his robe, and we all sat down. "I've tried everything I can think of," he said softly.

"I know that, John," Vicky said. "Tell Hugh what you think."

I hadn't been able to think of Tennant as a capable defense attorney until he turned then and looked at me, eyes somber, sincere, voice changing slightly, becoming deeper and more resonant. "I have defended twenty-seven persons accused of capital crimes, Mr. MacReedy. My father was murdered. He was an attorney. He made a successful defense in a large civil suit. A week later the plaintiff went to my father's office and took out a gun and shot him as he sat behind his desk. You can say I am oversensitized to murder. And to murderers. Though I am, in theory, opposed to capital punishment. I feel that murder is the one unforgivable crime. And thus I have never undertaken the defense of any person I have felt to be guilty. Twice I have discovered, late in the game, that my client had deceived me. I could not withdraw. I finished the defense in each case, and did my best. I number Alister Landy among the other twenty-five, among those persons innocent of the crime of which they have been accused."

I stared at him. "You believe that?"

"With all my heart. With all my experience, and with what intelligence I have been able to bring to bear. He didn't kill that girl."

"But won't anybody listen to you?"

"I'm not in what you would call an impartial position, MacReedy. The appeals I have made are classified as professional. Also there is a tragic coincidence. Two years ago I would have been able to speak confidentially to the Governor. He was a close personal friend who respected my opinions. We were of the same political party. Now the man in the State House is a political enemy. There is no way I can get a further stay of execution."

"Why are you so certain Alister is innocent?"

"Aside from the fact that I do not think he is that practiced a liar, there is one great logical flaw. The state claimed premeditation, basing it on the supposed theft of the knife. On most intelligence tests Alister nearly runs off the scale. Intelligence of that high order is capable of careful planning.

Were it premeditated, there would have been no such errors as there were."

"But he did make a terrible mistake!" Vicky cried.

"Yes. But he was badly rattled then. He found the smear of blood on the car seat. He removed it. He didn't report it. He suspected it was blood. He was frightened. At my advice, he admitted his actions on the stand. I should never have let him take the stand. It was a tactical error."

"What did he do?"

"He did well until Milligan made him angry. Then he became arrogant, noisy, derisive. He offended the jurors, insulted the court. It made a very bad impression."

"Let me ask a question, Mr. Tennant. Do you like him?"

"Like him? Feel affection for? I have to say no. I respect the quality of his mind. I think I understand him."

"He's easy to hate," I said.

"What are you getting at?" Vicky asked.

"Mr. Tennant knows what I'm getting at. He believes Alister innocent. So somebody is guilty. So somebody framed him—with the blood and the knife and pocketbook, and maybe with the tire tracks. Somebody hated him. There has to be a reason."

"I went into that," John Tennant said tiredly. "I paid a private investigator. I questioned Alister and Vicky. There were no specific enemies, no one who would go to that length, at least as far as we could discover."

"How about that girl he went with?"

"Nancy Paulson? She'd gone with another boy before she went with Alister. But that was back when she had been sixteen," Vicky said. "That other boy, Robby Howard his name was, died. He was drowned at the lake where the Paulsons go in the summer. It was very tragic. She didn't go with anyone else until she started going with Al last year."

"I can't imagine him dating a girl."

"He had changed a lot, Hugh, really. And I think she was good for him. She's a very pretty girl. Sensitive and bright. High spirited too. She wouldn't take any of Al's arrogance. That was what their last scrap was about when they saw each other on Thursday."

"What does she think about all this?"

Vicky frowned. "It's hard to say really. There were only the two girls. Naturally the Paulsons took it very badly. They've been preaching hate to her. I heard that it took them a long time to bring her around. She couldn't believe it. I still don't think that way down in her heart she has managed to believe it. I saw her once on the street. She looked away. But before she looked away there was a funny little expression of—appeal. Maybe an appeal for understanding. I guess she doesn't have the courage to fight the whole world."

"Your investigator," I said to Tennant, "couldn't find any other boy friends?"

"None. Nancy is a very steady girl, very reliable. He came up with a lot of stuff about the kid sister. I couldn't use it. I wouldn't get any sympathy for my client by maligning the dead."

"What kind of stuff?"

"To be very frank, Mr. MacReedy—"

"Hugh."

"All right. Hugh. My name is John. To be frank with you, the young Paulson girl at age sixteen was sexually precocious. She was in her first year of high school. There'd been trouble about her in junior high. Apparently she had started very early. She wasn't as pretty as Nancy. She was considerably more—earthy in appearance. I can remember an excerpt from a report. One of the high school boys was willing to talk, provided his name was kept secret. I can't remember the exact words, but it goes something like this. 'Jane Ann Paulson would take on anybody. It was like she just didn't gave a damn. When we had dances sometimes four or five guys would take her out in the parking lot, one at a time. Everybody knew what was going on. Some of the college guys were getting it too. She was too young to go in the bars, and they'd pick her up in Dockerty's Drugstore. It was hushed up now, but one time she was gone for three days during the Easter vacation and police were looking for her and everything, but it turned out she was at the Alpha Delt House up on the hill with a couple of fellows who hadn't gone home for the vacation. I guess she couldn't have been over thirteen, but she looked anyway eighteen ever since she was just past twelve. She's built big, up here. The two college fellows were expelled and I guess Jane Ann's old man just about beat her tail off, but you couldn't change her. Not her. All they could have done was send her away to one of those schools, but the Paulsons wouldn't do that. I guess they thought it would look bad. I guess they didn't know just about everybody in the whole town knew all about Jane Ann.' "

"I remember the scandal at the school," Vicky said. "It was hushed up fast, the way those things are."

"She doesn't sound like the sort of kid that gets raped," I said. "It doesn't sound as though rape would be necessary."

"That would have been my only justification for bringing all that information up," Tennant said. "But it couldn't do enough good to outweigh the harm. By then the papers had made her out to be a sweet, simple, virginal child."

"And for some reason that is the way the town seems to remember her," Vicky said. "All the rest is forgotten."

I thought for a moment and said, "Would that kind of background give anybody a motive to kill her? Suppose it was a married man. Maybe she was pregnant."

"Not according to the autopsy."

"How about blackmail?"

"Not likely."

At that moment the two paint-smeared kids came up, and the boy said, "It's all done except where we can't reach so high."

"Okay, workers of the world. You two go clean your brushes under the hose faucet. I'll be along to finish. Pour your paint back in the big can I was using."

The kids hurried off. "If you both think he's innocent, there has to be a starting place. I want to help. Where's the right place? Should I talk to Alister?"

"I can arrange it. But you won't get anything out of him. He has—withdrawn a long distance. He's far away. Weren't you going to see him tomorrow, Vicky?"

"Yes. It's all set."

"You could go up together. I'll get on the phone and fix it. But you won't be able to see him at the same time. Just one visitor at a time for fifteen minutes apiece. Vicky, don't let seeing him make you too upset."

She nodded. I said, "Any other starting places?"

"Nancy Paulson, perhaps. If she'll talk to you. If her people will let her talk to you. But listen. Both of you. Don't start dreaming. Don't think you can make everything all right. And you, Hugh, don't stick your neck out. Perry Score, the Chief of Police over there in Dalton, and that Quillan, his only assistant, are symptomatic of everything that can be wrong with small town police. Perry can do no wrong so far as County Sheriff Turnbull is concerned. They could rough you up and get away with it."

"What do you need? I mean, assuming we can find anything."

"Any evidence or statement that can be construed as to constitute reasonable doubt. Then phone me at once. But I'm not—optimistic."

Chapter 4

I DROVE VICKY BACK TO DALTON. John Tennant's pessimism had depressed her. When she would look at me she would try to smile, but I saw that it was an effort. She sat close to me.

Four miles out of Dalton I pulled over to the side of the road. "What is it, Hugh?"

"Get out. Come with me. Show you something."

I walked her forty feet along the road to one of the concrete slabs. It was the last one we had poured on the job. "See that slab?"

"What about it?"

"Pouring that one finished the job. Word got around when they were ready to pour. We drove up. Everybody on the job threw their hats in, between the forms, and then they were covered up. Old custom on every concrete job. My hat is in there."

"That beat-up felt hat with the hole in the crown?"

"You remember it?"

"Of course."

"It was a different guy who wore it, Vick. A jackass type guy."

"I liked him."

"Until?"

"Yes, until. Then I stopped liking him and couldn't stop loving him."

"How about this version? Can you like this one?"

She looked up at me. "Yes."

We kissed. A few cars hooted. We went back to the wagon. "So you all throw your hats in there."

"And then we go get drunk. A ritual. A duty. There are usually a minimum of three fist fights and two crap games. I won over four hundred bucks that day. The next day, all hung over, I started winding up the inspection and acceptance reports. And in the afternoon I was ordered out."

"You were glad to go?"

"I wanted to stay. But I felt helpless about ever talking to you."

"Let's not go back to that. Let's not think about that. Do you know what I want to do? I want to go to the apartment and finish the packing and get out of that old house and get away from Mrs. Hemsold."

We went back and packed hastily, efficiently. She had been saving Alister's things until last. She had not wanted to touch his things. I packed his stuff. Many books and notebooks. Not many clothes. And none of the stuff you would expect a college kid to own. Books in four languages. I couldn't learn much about him, learn anything that I hadn't known. But I did find a picture. It slid halfway out of a ponderous text written in Ger-

man. I sat on my heels and looked at it. Head and
shoulders of a blond girl smiling into the camera,
squinting slightly against the sun. It was a good
face, not quite formed into maturity—but there
was a clarity about it, that sort of honesty you
associate with the early Ingrid Bergman, and with
the pre-Rainier Kelly.

I took the picture out to Vicky in the kitchen.

"That's Nancy," she said.

"How could he have a girl like this one?"

"You don't understand these things. This one is
strong. Or gives promise of growing up to be
strong. And she can see things and understand. Al
is handsome, you know. But underneath there is
the helplessness, if you can see it. A woman can see
it easier. He has the almost traditional inability of
the professor type, inability to cope with the world
you and I know. She saw that."

"Okay," I said. "Inability. Take Einstein. That
was genius and he was probably more unaware of
the world around him than most, but there was
sweetness too."

"And sweetness in Al, but hidden way down."

I looked at the picture again. "This looks like all
girl."

"It is just a little deceptive. That picture makes
her look more outgoing than she is. Maybe that's
why he liked it best. There is a sort of timidity
about her. A wariness. As if she felt she had to
walk lightly and not make too much fuss."

"Parents?"

"I don't know. It seemed like a nice close family,
except for the trouble Jane Ann was giving them.
But you can't tell. Maybe my father wore a differ-

ent face for the outside world. Hugh, I can understand Al and Nancy because I can understand my
father and mother. In a lot of ways he was like
Alister. Ludicrous things would happen. He would
go into the bedroom in the middle of the day to
change his shoes. Then he would fall into a habit
pattern and, while his mind was working on something else, he would undress and put on pajamas
and go to bed and then realize that it was still
bright daylight so something must be wrong. My
mother had all the peasant strength he needed."

"This girl is a peasant?" I asked, looking at the
picture again.

"In reference to Al, yes. Square, strong little
hands. Strong body. Broad feet to plant firmly on
the ground. I'd say so."

"I'll hold onto this a while. Maybe it will
help."

We finished packing. There was no furniture. I
loaded all the cartons into the wagon, aware that
Mrs. Hemsold was watching every trip I took.
When the wagon was full, we put the rest of the
stuff into her Chevy coupé.

Mrs. Hemsold made her timed arrival just as
Vicky was making a last check to see that nothing
had been forgotten. The aged face was bright with
malice.

"*If* you don't mind, Miss Landy, I want to look
around before you leave and see if there's any damage to my property."

Vicky looked at her quite calmly and held out
the key. "Go right ahead, Mrs. Hemsold."

The old woman was aching for a fight. Vicky's
calm reaction seemed to irritate her. "I'm glad

you're leaving today. I didn't want to have to tell you that this man can't stay here with you. This is a decent house in a decent neighborhood."

Vicky seemed to grow taller. Her eyes flashed once. When she spoke her tone was still calm. "We haven't much time, Mrs. Hemsold. Suppose you just check for any damages. I'll mail you a forwarding address when I'm settled."

Mrs. Hemsold went in. We could hear her stumping indignantly about. I smiled at Vicky and told her she was a lady.

"If you could hear what I'm thinking, you wouldn't say so."

The old woman came out and complained about a burn on the counter top in the kitchen. Vicky informed her that the burn had been there when she had moved in. We went to the two cars. I looked back. The old woman was staring at us, implacable as weather, rigid as death.

"Now where?" Vicky asked.

"Out of town for you, I think. I know Charlie Staubs would take you at the MacClelland if I asked, but I don't want to put him on the spot, and I don't think it would be good for you. The stuff you'll need is in your car. I'll put all this other stuff into storage in Warrentown as soon as I get a chance. You follow me and I'll find a place for you."

I checked from time to time in the rear view mirror. She followed along. I remembered an area about fifteen miles north of Dalton where, at the conjunction of a superhighway and a main state road, a tourist area had been started three years before.

It had grown up a great deal. There were big glossy motels, restaurants, service areas. I picked what seemed to be the newest and the glossiest and she followed me into the lot.

"Here?" she said. "It isn't what I—"

"Hush! Look, you have a nice new name. Virginia Lewis. That'll fit the initials on your suitcase. I'm your fiancé."

I got her settled in. I watched the desk clerk carefully. There was no flicker of extra interest. I arranged for a room for a week. It was in the end of a wing far back from the road. The room was large, clean, impersonal, handsome. The rear door opened out onto a back garden. The bath with its pebbled glass shower stall looked as efficient as a comptometer. The towels were fluffy, the rugs deep. I suspected that it was more than she had wanted to pay, but she wouldn't let me help. I hoped she wasn't aware of all the reasons why I had insisted on this sort of place, and on the change of name. When the time of execution drew close, the ghouls would gather again. *Victoria Landy waits in hopeless tears as the hour draws closer. Sister of executed murderer hysterically proclaims his innocence on day of execution.* As an extra precaution I made certain that her car was parked so the plates couldn't be read from the highway. They were shiny new plates. I guessed that she had traded in the Ford the moment the state was through with it.

And also I wanted her to be in just such a cool, impersonal place when he was killed. This room had no rough edges, no place where memories could cling.

After she was unpacked there was still some warmth in the October afternoon, so we went out to the back garden and sat on white lawn chairs near a high cedar hedge.

She said slowly, "I think this was exactly right, Hugh. I feel a little apart from myself. Virginia Lewis doesn't have any problems. She's brand new. It would be nice, wouldn't it, if, as a sort of extra service, they had a brain surgeon here, and a nice refrigerated bank of clean unused brains. Then they could take this tired one out and put a new one in and make the stitches neat, and when I came out of the anesthetic they could say, 'Now you are Virginia Lewis and you are a gay person and there is a long warm life ahead of you.'"

"So Virginia would be all girly and giggly and I couldn't love her."

"You have to have a somber woman?"

"Not somber. But with a few shadows here and there."

"Mrs. Hemsold would just adore Virginia Lewis."

"Speaking of Mrs. Hemsold, I saw an antidote just up the street. The sign said package store."

"Superb suggestion, Mr. MacReedy."

I left her there and walked to the liquor store. I bought gin and vermouth there, and one lemon in a grocery store, and two very lean and deadly and handsome cocktail glasses in a gift shop. Back in the room the ice tinkled in the pitcher. The cold cocktail was pale in the glasses. The drops of lemon oil floated on the surface. I carried the drinks out. In a toast without words, the rims of the glasses made a bright tick as they touched.

"It *is* an antidote," she said a few moments later.

"Proposition. Be Virginia Lewis tonight. There's nothing we can do. Tomorrow you can be Vicky again."

She agreed quite solemnly. We drank until it was too cool to stay outside. We went in and split what was left in the pitcher. I talked and talked. The look of the Spanish landscape. The poverty of the people. The international set near Malaga. The self-importance of the Army Engineers.

Then she put a short coat on and we walked up the road in the night. Cars rushed by us as we walked on the shoulder. The restaurant was good, and the steaks were good. We walked back and I said good night to her at her doorway. She had unlocked the door. She took me by the wrist, her fingers cold, and tugged me toward her, through the open door into the dark room. We kissed hard and hungrily, and then she leaned against me for a little time and cried with hardly any sound at all. I knew how easy it would be. I knew how much I wanted her. But the old debt was large and it had to be paid, and trust can wither in morning light. I told her good night and drove back to Dalton and had a nightcap and went to bed.

State Prison is on the eastern boundary of the small industrial city of Mercer. It is in an area of freight yards, sidings, truck terminals, small chemical plants. The air has a smoky, acrid stench. The prison is big and the high concrete walls enclose a big area. It is a maximum security prison and the guard posts atop the walls are closely spaced. Directly across from the main gate is a cinder parking lot. The day was gray, but even the brightest of sunlight would have done little to change the look of gloom.

Vicky had been very silent on the ninety-mile drive. We arrived on time. I parked and walked across the road to the main gate. From the parking lot I had seen guards on catwalks leaning on the railing, looking into the compound. As we reached the gate I heard the deep roar of an excited crowd. For a few moments I could not identify the familiar sound. Then came a cadence that identified it to me. *Hold that line! Hold that line!* It was familiar, yet not familiar, because here was no intermingling of female voices. This was deeper, hoarser, angrier—more of an animal sound.

I talked through a small square cut into metal to the gate guards. They checked identity by phone to the office of the Guard Captain and then let us both inside the outer gate. We had to walk in turn through a narrow gate which I suspected was some sort of metal-detection device. We waited there until a guard came to get us. When he arrived they opened the inner gate with a pneumatic hiss. It was controlled from above, perhaps from the guard tower over the main gate.

The man who got us was elderly, slow-moving. His uniform was tight across the shoulders and shiny with age. Inside the compound the yelling was louder.

"Where is the game?" I asked.

"The field is over behind D Block," he said. "It ain't regulation so we got our own ground rules."

He took us to the Guard Captain's office. I saw men sitting in the afternoon sun, their backs against cell block walls, other men working at a big oval flower bed, taking out bulbs and putting them in flat wooden boxes. A railroad siding came into the prison through a large closed gate off to our right.

The anteroom of the Captain's office had the bored, weary smell of any police station in the world. There were two girlie calendars and some dusty framed pictures of groups of officials.

The elderly man said to a young clerk at a corner desk, "All cleared for a Landy visitor?"

"Just took the call. It's okay."

The old man turned to me. "You wait here, mister. It's just one at a time." She gave me a quick frightened smile and they left. I was left alone on a hard bench, hearing the hesitant clack of the clerk's typewriter, and the distant roar of crowd excitement.

"You get to see him, when she's through," the clerk said. "It's all fixed. But it's special. Usually only relatives."

I nodded. He typed some more. Then he stopped and said, "I hear the kid is taking it good so far. Lots of times they take it good right up to maybe an hour, two hours before the deal. Then they go nuts. They moved him yesterday into one of the bird cages."

"Bird cages?"

"Over there they keep you in a cell, see? If you got the lawyers working for you, maybe you are in the cell a year. Then you run out of appeals. So they leave you there until maybe a week, ten days before you're due. Then they move you to a bird cage where you got eyes on you night and day. The cages are on the top floor, see? Once since I been here all four were full. Now he's the only one up there."

I waited. Twice guards walked through the anteroom and into the inner office, giving me quick incurious glances. I wondered if I could smoke. I saw gray butts flattened against the dusty floor and I smoked two cigarettes. I had just finished the second one when she was brought back. There is a sisterhood of grief, of anguish, in which all women go apart from you and you cannot reach them. There is an habitual posture which makes you think of war drawings, of widows and refugees, of exile. She sat on the bench, shoulders hunched high, head lowered, handkerchief held to her eyes with both hands, body trembling. Despite the gay clothes she had worn, perhaps in an effort to cheer Alister, she could have been in rags, a peasant cloth over her head, knotted under her chin, bare brown feet dusty from roads that had been too long.

"Come along," the elderly guard said to me.

Bird cage was a good word. There were no windows in the room. Fluorescence was white glare. Three of the walls of his cage were heavy woven wire, the fourth a bare wall painted an unpleasant glossy green. Two guards played cards at a small table against a wall twenty feet from the cage. I was permitted to approach to a point six feet from the cage. The elderly guard stood beside me. Alister stood inside the cage, gray fingers hooked into the wire, head lowered. He looked thirty years old.

"Al!" I said sharply. He gave the impression that you had to awaken him. His head lifted slowly. He looked at me. They were Vicky's blue eyes. I had not remembered that. They were dulled. Recognition came slowly, lighting the eyes to a point of intensity and immediacy and then fading back to dullness.

"I want to help," I said. "I need some leads." I realized I was speaking the way one speaks to the sick, the deaf or the wounded. The elderly guard said, "She talked at him the whole time. He didn't answer. They get this way. Punchy like. The brainy ones do."

One of the guards at the table said, "And this kid has a real big brain on him."

"Shut up, George," the elderly one said gently.

"He's sick," I said. "He's mentally ill. You can't go ahead and—"

"The court says he's sane, mister. He's just gone back inside himself. He's inside there, thinking."

"With that big brain," the guard at the table said.

"For God's sake, George."

"Al!" I said again. He didn't lift his head.

"A week from tomorrow he'll be over his troubles," the guard said.

"You better take me back," I said.

As we left I looked back. He still stood there, like the prey of a shrike impaled on a barb.

She had stopped crying. Her face was pale and

empty. We were taken to the gate and they let us out. We got into the car and I drove into the middle of the shabby city and turned south. When we were on the open road she said, "Immature."

"What?"

"I was, Hugh. Turning it into some kind of a movie plot. In comes the hero. The vital clue is found. The innocent boy is released. He walks out into the sunlight, and the birds are singing. But it isn't that way. It's all too late. They've killed him already."

"He could come back. It would take time."

"But you see," she said patiently, "neither you nor I have any real hope of doing anything. We try to cheer each other up. There are only so many hours and minutes and seconds left. Then they'll kill him and now maybe that's best. Maybe that's the only thing left to do with him now."

"Vicky!"

"And when they do, Hugh, it's the end of him, and it's the end of anything we could have had. I won't wish on you what I will become."

"Is that self-pity?"

"I don't know. I don't care."

We stopped at a place but she couldn't eat. I took her back to the motel. She didn't want me to stay with her. Her eyes looked almost as empty as his.

I went back to the Inn. There had to be some starting place. I looked at my watch. I saw the sweep second hand moving around and around. Each revolution took that much off his life. And off mine and off Vicky's.

Chapter 5

MONDAY THE SEVENTEENTH was bright again and warm, the air flavored with the nostalgia of Indian summer. I had found the road where the kids parked, where the body had been found five days after the murder. I had driven up College Street hill and past the campus and past the faculty houses beyond the campus and past the small farms, five miles along the asphalt county road. Then the road dipped and turned west, to follow the ambling line of Three Sisters Creek. Two hundred yards from the turn there was a dirt road that led toward the creek some two hundred feet away. I drove into the dirt road. By the time I had gone thirty feet I was out of sight of the county road. When I turned off the motor I was in stillness. There were bird sounds, and wind through dry leaves, and the muttering of the creek.

I got out of the car. Beer cans rusted among fallen leaves. Shards of broken glass glinted in the sun. It was not hard to imagine what it would be like at night. A trace of dash lights on chrome. Dim pulse of the bass on the radio, gargle of liquor from the nearly empty bottle, the rough deep voice of a boy trying to talk like a man, a girl's thin, empty and expected protests, and then the quickening oven-breathing, sleazy rustlings of nylon, and then, for the bolder ones, the hastily spread blanket and hip-thump against the wounding earth while girl eyes glaze at a sky of swarming stars. A cheap thirty-second taste of eternity.

I wandered toward the creek and after a time I heard voices. I found them, three boys in the twelve-year-bracket, sloshing and yelping in a black pool under high rock shadow, bright bikes discarded in sunlight.

They were brashly self-conscious about skipping school, and delighted to show me the exact place where the body had been found, along with descriptions too lurid to be possible. Their knowing language about the ways of the law was directly from any third-rate television script. One of them spotted a used flash bulb in the aspen patch and snatched it up.

"My dad says they ought to burn everybody that attacks girls even when they don't kill 'em."

"*My* dad says the chair is too easy for Landy."

"I'll betcha if they could have got him away from the cops they would have fixed him good."

Soon they became bored with me and went back to the pool. I walked to the car. I had read the account in the back issues of the Warrentown paper, the reconstruction of the crime. The girl had been killed at the spot where the body was found, some seventy feet from the tire tracks. From the way twigs had been broken, she had tried to run. The killer had caught her. It made the gruesome chase more real to see the place. But I could learn nothing new there. Nothing factual. From the results of Tennant's investigation, it was evident that Jane Ann was no stranger to this particular parking area, nor would she have been reluctant to come here. She would not have panicked and run from any normal advance. Some instinct had warned her, or perhaps the sight of the knife.

I found the Paulson address in the telephone book—88 Oak Road. I had remembered seeing that street sign somewhere near Maple Street, and found it quickly. It was the first cross street after you passed Mrs. Hemsold's house on Maple, going away from the square. The houses were smaller than the houses on Maple. They were frame houses and they were well maintained and looked comfortable. Eighty-eight was a brown house with yellow trim, two story and unpleasantly square. There were two red maples in the front yard, and a box hedge along the sidewalk. It looked to be exactly what it was, the home of the owner of a successful market, with mortgage that had dwindled methodically through the years. It had a look of immunity to the sort of disaster it had suffered. There should still be two daughters in the house to sprawl in front of television, to quarrel over clothes, to spend inane hours at the phone.

Before I had looked at the house I had stopped in at the market to take a look at Richard Paulson. I had taken my time over a small purchase. I had guessed that he was the man behind the meat counter and it was confirmed when I heard a customer call him by name.

He was a tall man with a long face and high color in his cheeks. His no-color hair was carefully and intricately combed so that it lay across the baldness of his head. His shoulders were narrow, his hands large and red. He was surprisingly thick in the middle, considering the gauntness of his cheeks. He wore his white apron with dignity, and as he worked his hands were deft. His eyes and his mouth were too small, and his nose was fleshy. He looked to be a coldly methodical man, and when he talked to customers his affability seemed forced and insincere. Watching him I thought I could understand a little more easily the reasons for Jane Ann's rebellion. He would be too harsh and too logical. And I wondered if Nancy's conformity was the result of a broken spirit. I could hear rigid moral platitudes coming from that coin slot mouth. It was odd to hear customers call him Dick. An equal number called him Mr. Paulson.

As I drove by the house I could see, in the geometric placement of the red maples, in the rigid clipping of the box hedge, in the unhappy squareness of the house itself, reflections of his personality.

It was a reasonable premise that Nancy would walk home from the high school. And the route she would take was obvious. I parked a block from the school. When the kids started coming out, I got out of the car and leaned against it. All the young girls looked alarmingly alike. Several times I was on the verge of speaking when I saw that I was mistaken. I glanced at the picture again to refresh my mind.

Finally I saw her and I was certain. She was with two other girls. They were talking animatedly and, like the others who had passed, they gave me sidelong glances as they came abreast and the other two changed their walks in subtle ways, making an instinctive offer of young bodies, a subconscious response to maleness that is as old as the race.

"Nancy?"

She was nearly by me. She stopped and turned sharply, frowning, head tilted slightly, then pretty face becoming bland and cool as she realized she did not know me.

"What do you want?" Her voice was pitched too high and it was slightly nasal.

"I want to talk to you for a minute."

The three of them stood there speculating, staring at me. "What about?"

"Is this yours?" I held the picture so she could see it.

"Where did you get that?" Indignation, tempered by the slight coyness of a young girl talking of her own photograph.

"I want to talk to you alone for a minute."

She spoke to her friends. "Wait up for me." They moved slowly down the block, looking back. Nancy came hesitantly toward me and stopped a cautious distance away.

"Where did you get that?"

"It was his."

"I know. There were only two. I've got the other one."

"I want to talk to you."

"I'm not allowed to talk to newspaper people."

"I'm not one of those."

"Then what do you want? Who are you?"

"I'm a friend of Vicky's."

Her face changed and she backed away. "I don't want to talk to you."

"Wait a minute. You don't want to talk to any friend of hers—or his?"

She backed further, lips compressed, shaking her head.

"You're going to run now, aren't you, Nancy? You'll run because you're afraid you'll find out he didn't do it."

That stopped her retreat. She looked dazed for a moment and then curiously indignant. "*Everybody* knows he did it!"

"Three of us know he didn't. Vicky, Mr. Tennant and myself. Four when you count Al."

She moved back toward me, not knowing she was doing so. "That's crazy. How could anybody *know*? He did it. Everybody knows he did it."

I took a chance. "Nancy, for a long time you *knew* he didn't do it. What changed you?"

"I was being silly when I thought that. My father explained—"

"Don't kid me, Nancy. This is a small town. You don't want to be unpopular. You don't want to be different. You want to believe just what everybody else believes. So it was too expensive for you to be loyal."

"It *wasn't* that way!"

"This is a good picture, Nancy. The photographer made you look very honest and very brave. So I made a mistake. I'm wasting my time. You're a good-looking kid but you're another gutless wonder. There's no point in asking you for any help. You're too concerned about what people might think."

I flipped the picture at her. It scaled through the air, struck her shoulder, fell to the sidewalk. She snatched it up. Her face was red. Her eyes were narrow and angry. I watched her walk away. It was a calculated risk. The young want desperately to conform, yet at the same time each one wants to feel unique and unswayed by public opinion. I counted twelve briskly indignant steps and thought I had lost. Then I saw the hesitation, saw her turn and look back at me. I looked away, snapped my cigarette into the road and opened the door of the wagon.

She came back slowly, stopped her usual wary distance away.

"What kind of help?"

"Don't waste my time, Nancy. Run off and play. Go sew up some doll clothes. This is business for grownups."

She stamped her foot. "What do you want me to do?"

"Something you haven't got the courage to do. Something very minor. Just meet me and talk to me with frankness and honesty and answer every question I care to ask you."

"But why?"

"We've got a very ridiculous idea, Nancy. We'd like to find out who really killed your sister."

"That's crazy talk! Al did it. It's all over now."

I looked directly at her and I waited until a woman carrying a shopping bag walked by us. "I'll tell you something not very many people know, Nancy. When a person is electrocuted, there's a problem of timing. Once when a notorious kidnaper was executed, they made a mistake."

"What are you—"

"Shut up and listen. They pulled the switch when his lungs were full of air. When that happens and the current hits, it makes a sound you can hear for four city blocks, a sound you can't ever forget. So they watch the chest and pull the switch at the end of an exhalation. When they do that to Alister a week from today, then it will be over, Nancy. And until they do that it isn't over."

Her eyes closed and she swayed, her face chalky. I moved toward her and caught her arm. She opened her eyes and moistened her lips and swallowed with an effort. She did not try to move away from me.

"There's—nothing I can tell you that will help."

"You can't know that. But if you can make yourself believe that, it will be a lot easier for you." I released her arm. "You can still run along with your friends. After next Monday you can start wondering if by talking to me you might have changed things. And you can wonder about that for all the rest of your life."

"I—can't talk to you now."

"Why not?"

"I have to go right home. I'll be a little late now. Mother gets frantic if I don't go right home. She's been that way ever since—it happened."

"But you can get out again?"

"Yes. But I have to be back by five-thirty."

"Can I pick you up somewhere?"

"No. No, I couldn't go anywhere in your car with you. I couldn't have anybody seeing me in a car with somebody."

"Where do you usually go?" I asked.

"Most of the time to Dockerty's Drugstore where all the kids go. Maybe I could talk to you in the park there, on one of the benches in the square."

"I'll wait for you."

She acted nervous and furtive. She started to turn away and turned back. "I don't care what people think, but my father—"

"You act scared of him."

"He's different than he was before."

"Will this make you feel better? Nobody has to know what we're talking about."

She looked relieved. She walked away, schoolbooks cradled in her arm, with only one quick, nervous, backward glance.

The bench I selected was not on one of the main cross paths. I sat and watched an enthusiastic and inept game of touch football. One small boy insisted on making his tackles legitimately until he caught a knee on his nose. The dismal sounds he made were audible after he was out of sight.

I saw her when she was a hundred yards away. She crossed the street, walking primly. She had changed to jeans and a red cotton flannel shirt. Her blond hair was tied into a high pony tail with blue ribbon. She walked more slowly, looking around until she spotted me, and then came toward me. Her walk seemed very self-conscious, very body-conscious, as though she was making a deliberate effort to suppress any movement that could call attention to breasts or hips. It was not a natural walk for a girl so pretty, so nicely built. It was a denial of the natural and unself-conscious pride she should have had.

As I had seen when I had talked to her near the school, she was not the girl of the picture. That special look of clarity was gone, as was the impression of imminent maturity. The murder had made growing up too expensive for her, and perhaps for reasons of self-preservation, she had slid back into the formlessness of adolescence, back into the random jungles.

She gave me a nervous nod and sat on the far end of the bench, as far from me as she could get, her face averted.

"I decided not to come," she said.

"Then why did you?"

She ignored the question. "I don't know who you are or anything. Maybe you're going to write a story about this. I don't see why I should talk to you. My father had to get the police to get men away from our house."

"I told you I'm a friend of Vicky's."

"Anybody could say that."

I took out my wallet, found the right card and handed it to her. It had my picture and thumbprint and physical description. The text, in both Spanish and English, said I was employed on the airfield project.

She studied it and handed it back. "What does it mean? That says in Spain."

"I'm on a vacation."

"You're awful tan."

"Nancy, I don't blame you for being suspicious. I'm in the construction game. I was on a road job near here. I met Vicky then. I didn't know she was in this trouble until I got back to Chicago. Then I came here. Maybe you're almost old enough to understand this. In one sense I'm almost glad of this trouble, because it gave me a good excuse to come back here and see her again."

She gave me a rare look of directness. "Do you love her?"

"Yes. And when I left before, I thought I'd never see her again. I gave her a bad time."

Her eyes widened. "You're *that* one!"

"Then you know about it."

"Not much about it. Just some things Al said. You made her unhappy. He said you took the life out of her."

"I've been sorry ever since, Nancy. Now I'm trying to help her."

She had me placed, and she seemed more at ease. "I don't see how anybody can change it now, Mr. MacReedy."

"I don't see how either. But I'm not closing my mind the way you are."

"I came here, didn't I? I'm willing to talk to you."

"It's good to see you mad instead of scared."

"I'm not scared."

"Then we'll talk. We'll talk like friends, Nancy. Maybe if you can act like a grownup we can be friends. You're eighteen years old. You aren't a child. I want us to talk together like a man and a woman. And I want us both to make one major assumption before we start. Let's assume Al is innocent."

"But—"

"It's the attitude a court of law is supposed to have. I think if we start that way, we may get farther. Forget that this town considers him some sort of a monster. You don't have to think that way because they do. Now—can you pretend?"

"I know the meaning of the word assumption," she said haughtily.

"Then we can start?"

She nodded nervously, and looked down at her hands. She seemed to relax a little, but not as much as I would have expected of a girl of eighteen. There was an odd wariness about her.

"You were in love with Alister."

"I—I thought I was."

"Your father explained to you how you really weren't."

"I guess so."

"And he told you you are too young to know what real love is."

"Y-Yes."

"But you don't really think he's right, do you?"

"I don't know. I guess so."

"Stop fencing, Nancy. What do you think of Alister?"

"He's—strange. He's not like other boys. He doesn't have any kind of line or anything. I—I met him in our back yard. He was watching a bird. He sort of wandered over, following it when it went from tree to tree. He was shy. He's very smart. It could scare you, the things he knows and how quick he learns things, but he wouldn't scare you the other way."

"What other way?"

"I mean he—he was different. Usually we had a good time. Only sometimes he'd get angry. I guess I'm not too bright. Not with his kind of brains. He needed somebody."

"Don't you think he still does?"

"But—"

"Nancy. Listen to me. Listen carefully. Can you really imagine him murdering Jane Ann?"

"My father says you can't ever tell—"

"A book by its cover. The hell with your father." She jumped as though I had slapped her. "I want to know what you think. What Nancy Paulson thinks. Do you think he had something twisted inside him that would let him do a terrible thing like that?"

"Well—Jane Ann was always teasing him."

"How?"

"Oh, in little ways. You know. Making him blush and get all confused. She was like that. She liked to do that to shy boys. Leaning up against them. Saying things that were almost dirty but not quite, and then laughing in a sort of wise way."

"So he could kill her because she teased him."

"Well, I kept thinking that maybe she sort of led him on. You know. And he got thinking about her. And then he was mad at me and he saw her walking and he picked her up and—Well, my father says that some men go out of their heads when they—"

"Did Alister ever kiss you?"

She looked at me and looked away, and her blush was really Victorian. "Yes," she said in a small voice. "Lots of times. But that was all."

"Did he act like he was going to go out of his head?"

"No. He wasn't like that. And he was polite. He didn't get—funny or anything."

"You're a better looking girl than your sister was. You're a more exciting looking woman."

"Don't—Please don't say things like that."

"Most girls like to hear that sort of thing."

"I don't. If you talk like that I'm going home."

"I'm not making any pass at you. I'm trying to figure you out. If kissing you didn't make Alister lose control, is it likely to think he'd lose control kissing your sister?"

"She was different."

"How do you feel about her? I mean what did you think about the way she acted with boys?"

"I don't know what you mean," she said, though I knew she understood me.

"I don't know what you kids call it. When I was in high school we'd call her a girl that went all the way."

"Don't talk dirty like that."

"Look, Nancy. I am *not* talking dirty. Somebody killed your sister. We're pretending it wasn't Alister. And we know it wasn't some person just passing through. The blood on the car and the buried knife and purse rule that out. What did you think about the way she acted, the things she did?"

Nancy lowered her head. I had to move closer to hear her. "I thought it was awful. It made me ashamed, all the time. It made the boys worse because they thought I was the same way. I never was. I never will be. I don't want to do nasty things. Al didn't either. We talked about her. He said it wasn't really the way she was. He said it was a protest. She was so nice when she was little. We had so much fun. Then it all changed. I guess I'm terrible. Now everybody pretends they can't remember the way she was with boys. And it's like a weight off me. I can't feel as bad about her as I ought to feel. She was my sister. I don't want to be glad she's dead. But she was going to keep right on doing terrible things. My father beat her. It didn't change anything. He'd beat her so hard it would scare mother and me. But she'd go out a window. She'd sneak out. It didn't matter to her. She'd cry when he hurt her and afterward she'd laugh. Nothing mattered. She'd talk dirty to me until I was so ashamed I'd cry, and then she'd laugh at me. In school I knew everybody was looking at me when I walked down the hall, and I was ashamed."

"When did she start being like that?"

"It was in the summer. Let me try to remember when. She would have been seventeen this last summer. So it was five summers ago. When she was twelve. At the lake. Morgan's Lake. We've always gone there. The Mackins own half of it. They live just down the street from us—on the corner of Oak and Venture. There's a boathouse and a sort of upstairs to it. You get up there by a ladder. My father and Mr. Mackin keep gear up there. My father went up there after something and Jane Ann and a boy were up there." She lowered her head and flushed. "They had taken their swim suits off. Even when she was twelve Jane Ann was—you know. Big." And she half indicated what she meant by the fragment of a gesture toward her own breasts. "The boy was from across the lake. His name was Danny something. She said they were playing doctor. My father whipped the boy so bad there was a lot of trouble about it, but everybody knew he was right to do it. He whipped Jane Ann too. And made her stay inside the camp for a whole month. She cried a lot at first and then she got mean. I think that was when she started to change."

"And after a while your father couldn't do anything with her."

"That's right. They talked—my mother and father—about sending her to one of those schools. Mr. Score, the Chief of Police, said they should after that time she stayed at that fraternity house, but my father said it would have been a disgrace to the family."

"There was a boy you went with when you were up there at the lake, wasn't there?"

She turned her head quickly and looked directly at me. It was a look of alarm. "Robby. Robby Howard. They said I was too young to have a boy friend. I was sixteen. He was nice. He was like—"

"Like Alister?"

"I was going to say that. Yes. Like Alister, I guess. Shy, and he didn't try to get funny or anything. And he was drowned. It took a whole day to find him. They tried to make me look away but I saw him on the dock before they covered him up. He was black, his skin." She shuddered visibly.

"How did he drown?"

"They thought it was a cramp. He was a wonderful swimmer. Nobody saw him and they didn't know where it happened and that's why it took so long to find him. It is a little lake. I used to have to sneak away to see him. It made me feel guilty and funny. Like I was being like Jane Ann."

"You were serious about him?"

"I thought all of the world had ended. We had a crazy idea. We talked about it. About running away. He was seventeen. He knew all about radios. He had built a lot of them. He looked older than seventeen, we thought. He could get a job in a repair shop. He found out you can get married in Georgia when you're sixteen without anybody's permission. They didn't want me to see him, and we thought it was the only thing we could do."

"Had you thought of marrying Alister?"

"We sort of took it for granted. We talked about it like it was going to happen. I don't know when we decided we would exactly. It was going to happen after he graduated. The University of Illinois was going to give him a research fellowship thing. I could take my last year of high school there, and then go into the university. He wanted me to do that, and I said I would but I didn't see why I should."

"Did your family know about the plan?"

"Oh, no!"

"What do you think they would have thought of it?"

"My father would have said no. And all that time I was wondering if I had the courage to do it anyway. I think I would have."

"Did you think at all about the physical side of marriage?"

"I don't want you to talk like that."

"Nancy, please. I'm not trying to play games. This all may be important. I don't know just how, but it may be a factor in this whole thing. I'm a stranger. You probably won't see me again. I'm not making any kind of a pass. I'm in love with Vicky Landy, and I've done enough living to know that any other girl from here on in is of no use to me in any physical sense. I asked you this question. What did you think about the physical side of marriage?"

"I—I thought about it. A lot, I guess. I didn't know how it would be. I mean I know what happens, but I couldn't imagine it being done to me. It scared me. It seems so—so nasty. A terrible thing. Jane Ann kept wanting to do it. I couldn't understand how she could want that. She said it was fun; but I don't think it was really for her, because so many times she would be so sour and moody. I— guess I just hoped that Alister would be gentle and not scare me and not want to do it very often, so maybe then I could pretend to him it was all right."

"Nancy, I'm not criticizing you, really. But that isn't a healthy or normal way to think. There are a lot of girls and women who think the way you do. And a few men. Something must have caused that attitude."

"You're not right. The other kind of people are dirty."

"They're normal, honey. How do your parents feel about all this?"

"I don't know. I don't want to think about it."

"You weren't found under a cabbage leaf, you know."

"Stop it! I don't let myself think about that."

"Because it's nasty, I suppose. Has your mother lectured you about this nastiness?"

"No. Never."

I studied her closely and decided that she was not lying. This girl would make someone a wonderfully frigid wife. The emotional block was so pronounced that only superhuman patience could ever create a natural relationship. An initial queasiness had perhaps been intensified by the waywardness of the sister, by the severity of the beatings her sister was given, by the aura of innuendo in her social contacts with her contemporaries. Yet this did not seem enough. Had Jane Ann been the elder sister, it would seem more reasonable. Many nuns are the younger sisters of dissolute women. And the children of drunkards are often highly moral. I could not decide what had twisted this girl. And, also, I could not help but think, in the romantic tradition—or perhaps hope is the better word—that the kink in her emotions was something that could be unknotted by the right word, the right gesture. As in the sexual symbolism of Sleeping Beauty.

She took advantage of my silence to say, "I don't see how this has anything to do with whether Alister did it."

"Perhaps it doesn't. Let's try another approach.

It came out at the trial that you and Alister had quarreled on Thursday night. Did you have a date with him for Friday?"

"Yes, but we broke it after the fight."

"Was it a bad fight?"

"Not very bad. It was mostly silly. He started talking about this town in that funny way of his, saying how it was such an awful, narrow, little place, full of prejudice and jealousies and tribal rites. I said it was my home and I liked it. He said if I couldn't see it for what it was, I was blind or stupid or both. We—went on from there."

"Did your parents approve of your dating him two nights in a row?"

"I don't think my father liked it. I heard him and my mother arguing. She said I was eighteen and he couldn't keep me locked up. I don't think they had anything against him. He was always polite to them. But I knew him better and I could see that it was—like a pose. Like he was playing a game. Like he was trying to be the kind of boy they wanted me to go with."

"How about other boys? Were there any others?"

"Oh, no! Just Robby and Alister."

"But other boys must have tried to date you."

"They try all the time. But they're a different kind. I know what they're thinking about all the time. Now we're talking about *that* again. I don't like to. It makes me feel all crawly."

"Then we'll change quick. Would Jane Ann have gotten into a car with a stranger?"

"I don't know. Even though she was the way she was, I don't think so. But maybe if he was young and it was a nice car—you know."

"Was there anybody around town who was after her? Maybe somebody older and pretty unattractive. Maybe a village idiot type."

"No. There wasn't anybody like that. I don't know of anybody like that."

"What happened to her things afterward? Maybe she had a diary or letters or something."

"The police looked for things like that when she was missing, before they found her. They thought she had run away. I think my father thought so too. But I didn't think so."

"Why not?"

"She didn't take the things from her locker at school. I guess I better explain that. After she started doing bad things, my father wouldn't give her any allowance. I get an allowance and I have to buy my clothes and personal things out of it. He wouldn't let my mother buy her anything pretty. But I guess she made boys buy her presents. She had wonderful sweaters and skirts and things in her locker. She'd always get to school early enough so she could pick an outfit out of her locker and go change in the girls' room. Then after school she would change back into her other clothes. She couldn't wear any of those things home. Once she brought a dress home and when she put it on my father asked her where it came from and she wouldn't tell him, so he ripped it and called her a whore."

"Did she tell you who bought her the things?"

"No. I guess they were from the Sheridan boys. They have more money. She kept jewelry and perfume and lipstick in her locker. Afterward the school opened the locker and sent all those things home. I knew she probably hadn't run away, because I knew that when she closed her locker on Friday all those things were in there. I was with her. I had to ask her something. I forget what it was. If she was going to run away, she would have packed up those pretty things and maybe left them off with a girl friend. After school closes on Friday you can't get back into the lockers until Monday."

"What happened to the clothing?"

"My father gave it all away. My mother thought I could use some of the sweaters, but I couldn't have worn them."

"Who got the stuff?"

"My mother thought we could save it for the church rummage sale; but my father took it all, the pretty things and the things she wore at home, and drove over to Warrentown and gave it to the Salvation Army."

"How did she manage when she had a date and wanted to dress up?"

"She kept other clothes over at a girl friend's house. Ginny Garson. She's—just like Jane Ann was. Ginny was her best friend. I've seen Ginny wearing some of her things, so I guess she just kept them. They were about the same size, but Ginny is dark."

"She didn't go over there and change that night she was killed?"

"No. She thought she had a date and then she didn't and I guess she was mad about it. There wasn't any need to dress up. She was going up the hill to see another friend of hers. Not a very good friend. Ann Sibley. She's the daughter of one of the professors at the college. Ginny had a date that night."

"You didn't tell the police that you were pretty certain she hadn't run away."

"No. But it wouldn't have made any difference. They were hunting all over anyway. I guess if they'd found the money first instead of later they—" She gasped and put her hand over her mouth.

"What money?"

"I can't tell you. I promised I wouldn't tell anybody."

I had to argue, plead and browbeat her, and tell her how important it could be to Alister before she consented to tell me about it. "My father found it. It was a long time later. It was while the trial was on. You see if the police had found it when they searched her room they would have known she hadn't run away. My father was like a crazy man when he found it. It was by accident. The house is small. He was going to change her room into an office where he could work on the books and charge accounts from the market. The trial was terrible for all of us. When it was recessed over a week end we came back and we all tried to keep busy. There were so many reporters calling we had to have the phone disconnected. And the Chief sent Barney Quillan over to keep people away from the house. That week end my father decided he would carry her bureau up to the attic to make way for the desk he was going to put in her room. He thought it would be easier to carry if he took the drawers out first. That was the way he found it. It was in one of

those heavy reddish envelopes that was thumb-
tacked to the back of the drawer, so you had to take
the drawer out to get to it."

"Was there much?"

"He talked so loud to my mother I couldn't help
hearing. He made me go to my room but I didn't
shut the door all the way. It was eight hundred and
something. Eight hundred and twenty, I think. He
called it whoremoney, and the wages of sin. He
carried on for a long time. It hurt him very badly. I
don't know what ever happened to it. I guess he
used it in the business. Or maybe he used it on the
funeral bill. He made me promise that I would
never tell anyone. He said it was a disgrace."

"Don't you think he should have told the police?
Maybe they would have started looking for someone else."

"Oh, no! Everybody knew Alister did it."

And again I had run into the blank wall. I sighed
and said, "Where do you think the money came
from?"

"I guess the boys gave it to her. I guess she asked
them for it and they would give it to her before
she'd let them—do anything. Like they gave her
the sweaters and things."

We had talked a long time. She had to leave. She
was becoming very nervous about the time and she
kept glancing across the square toward the Paulson Market. It was obscured by trees but she kept
looking in that direction. I asked her how I could
contact her again if I had more questions. She was
reluctant at first, then told me that if I really *had*
to talk to her, I could park near the school. She
would see my car and meet me here at this same

bench a half hour later, or another bench close by if somebody was using this one. I wasn't to talk to her or even look at her when I parked near the school. She said that if her father ever found out she was talking like this, and particularly if he should find out she had talked about the money, he would whip her. He would be angry. She was frightened of being whipped. One time he had whipped Jane Ann too hard. It had done something to her back. She had to wear a sort of corset thing for six weeks. The doctor had been very angry at her father. Dr. Farbon. He had been their family doctor for years, but he said the wrong things, and so her father had changed over to Dr. Higel, the new man.

She hurried away into the threat of dusk, and when she was far away, she looked back hastily and furtively. Her constricted walk was a sad thing to watch. Poor scared lamb in a wolf-infested world. Panicky virgin, running headlong from herself.

I walked across the green to the Inn and, using the phone booth in the rear of the entrance hall, I called John Tennant in Warrentown. I caught him just as he was leaving for a cocktail party. I told him about the money, about how I had found out about it, and I asked him if it was sufficient new evidence on which he could base a request for an appeal.

First he made some comments about Richard Paulson. He used not a single profane word, but he traced the probable ancestry and probable demise of Mr. Paulson with both fervor and emphasis. Then he said, "Hugh, it's interesting. It's provocative. It's a new fact. But it isn't enough. Paulson will deny it. He'll make the daughter say she was lying. I may try to use it as a last forlorn hope if I have to. But there should be more. I suddenly have a lot more respect for your amateur talents. My boy didn't dig that morsel up. How about I send you somebody down to help out?"

"Let me find out first if I need somebody. I've got a starting point now. And a new contact to make. One of Jane Ann's girl friends. Her best friend."

"Good hunting, Hugh."

I drove to the motel. Vicky was still depressed. But as I told her what I had learned, I saw the rebirth of hope in her eyes. I wondered if I should have told her. Perhaps it would have been more kind to keep it to myself. It lifted her up a little bit, only to give her further to fall. She was almost gay at dinner. Then I told her I had work to do, and I went back to Dalton.

Chapter 6

THE GARSON HOME was the nearest thing to being on the wrong side of the tracks that the town of Dalton could provide. It was on the Warrentown-Dalton road, about ten blocks from the Paulson home. Successive widenings of the highway had placed it too close to the road. There was a small

woodworking mill on one side of it, a bar and grill
on the other. Directly across the road was a new-
looking farm implement dealership, with show-
room night lights gleaming on flanked tractors,
and intricate accessories.

I had been told the Garson home was directly
across from the implement place. I parked on the
wide apron in front of the implement place, and
waited for a hole in the traffic so that I could walk
across.

There was a narrow porch across the front of the
house. The yard was bare. Oncoming headlights
illuminated a tire swing hanging from a tree close
to the corner of the porch. As I had walked across
the road I had heard low male voices on the dark
porch, and the clink of bottle neck on glass.

I walked up the first two steps and paused when
a man asked, with the faked belligerence of someone who has had too many bill collectors come,
"Something you want?"

I could make them out dimly. Two sitting on a
couch, one slouched against the porch railing, facing them. The three faces were turned toward
me.

"I'm trying to locate Ginny Garson. Is this where
she lives?"

"She lives here, but she's out some place. She's
my kid. What do you want to see her about? School
trouble?"

"No, it's not that. It's about the Landy case."

"You the law?"

"No, I—I want to get a story."

"You come too late, buster. They got her story.
Took pictures, too. Made her get her swimming

suit on and for one of them they took her across the road and the fellow had her making out like she was driving one of them tractors over there. It's going to come out right after they burn that Landy son of a bitch. *Cora!*"

He called so loudly it startled me. A woman came to the door. She stood inside the screen. The light was behind her. It shone through her thin dress. She had massive hips and thighs, a long neck, scrawny shoulders. She spoke in a tired whining tone. "I can God damn well hear you, Jerry, without you yell like a crazy man."

"Shut up," he said amiably, "and tell me what is the name of that story that magazine is putting out about Ginny next month."

"That story it's called 'He Killed My Best Girl Friend' and it comes out in a magazine called *True Emotion* that's one of my favorites."

"The thing I remember about it, they wanted to give Ginny twenty-five bucks for a release thing, but I dickered 'em up to fifty bucks."

"And you give her ten and me ten and you lost the whole thirty down to Bristol's in the pitch game on Saturday night."

"Shut up, Cora. This fellow here, he's another one of those magazine fellows. How much you giving out for a release? Ginny, I bet you she could tell you some stuff she didn't tell those others."

I had gotten into a trap without meaning to, and it seemed easier to let it slide. "This is just speculation, Mr. Garson. I don't work for a magazine. I'd do it and then try to sell it and give her part of the money if I do."

"How much?"

"Maybe there isn't any story left. I'd have to talk to her."

"Where is she, Cora?"

"I don't know how the hell you think I can keep track. I got five littler than her and this all the time washing and cleaning up and cooking and you never lift a hand to—"

"Knock it off before I come in there and kick your teeth in, woman."

She turned away from the door abruptly, indignantly. One of the other men spoke for the first time. He had a low, slow voice with a Deep South tinge. "I see the Quarto kid pick her up about seven in that chopped Ford of his. They was a mess of them in the car. They hang around that Big Time Burger Drive-In about five mile east on this here road. It's on the left. You can't miss it. The Ford, it's yellow and it's chopped and it's got a fish tail and chrome blower pipes. But just ask any of the kids out there. They all go out there. My boy, he's out there I betcha, if he hasn't got hisself killed off driving out there at a hundred and ten miles an hour. His driving like to drive the old lady nuts. You just ask out there. You can't miss it."

"And before you do any story," Mr. Garson said blusteringly, "you're going to put down in writing all notarized just what she gets paid if you sell it."

I thanked them and turned to leave.

"Hey!" the third man said. "Hold it!" I turned back. "I was wondering why you sounded familiar and then you turned and the light hit your face. Your name ain't MacReedy is it? By God, I'm sure it is. You was an engineer on that road job three years ago. And I was working for the paymaster. I'd know you any place. And hey now! Jerry, this joker is MacReedy and I remember now he was running around with the Landy bitch."

The atmosphere changed quickly. I was annoyed at myself for trying to take the easiest way out. The odds were good that at least one of the men on that porch had worked on the road job. Labor remembers the bosses.

"And now you write stories," Garson said softly.

"Well, I just—"

He got up, tucked his thumbs in his belt and came rolling toward me with all the trite stylized belligerence of the barroom hero. His friend got up from the couch. The southerner pushed himself free of the railing and drifted along with them.

"What do you want to talk to my little girl about, MacReedy?"

"I told you I wanted her story on the Landy case. You brought up the magazine angle."

"And you let me keep thinking I was right, wise guy. What are you after?"

"The truth, Mr. Garson. Your daughter may know something that will help."

"Help your girl friend's brother? Help that sex fiend killer? You ought to be run the hell out of town."

He was moving closer, gaining courage from his friends. A bluff couldn't hurt anything. "We've already got enough new information so that Tennant is reopening the case, Garson."

"Nuts!"

"I'm telling you the tru—"

I barely saw the sucker punch coming. I ducked it in time. I backed down the steps and into the yard. They came down the steps and the two friends drifted out onto the flank. I turned and moved quickly, crossed the road and started to get into my car. I knew the trouble he could cause if I hurt anybody on his property. One of them had come after me, running in deadly silence. He yanked me around by the arm, swinging at the same instant. It was the southerner. The blow hit me high on the cheek bone, driving me back against the wagon and lighting up the night sky for an instant. He trusted that punch too much. He tried it again. I slapped his arm down and to the side and heard his quick suck of breath as his hand hit the frame of the wagon between the windows. I pushed him away to gain room, and hit him in the pit of the stomach. He doubled over and I slapped the side of his head as hard as I could. It made a noise like a pistol shot and knocked him down. The thin intensity of his yell came from the bursting pain of a ruptured eardrum.

The other two moved in on me, one from each side. I took a fist on the throat and felt as though I might strangle. Garson's co-ordination was poor, his belly swollen with ten thousand beers. I put arm, shoulder, back and hip into one right hook that couldn't have traveled over ten inches. It made a sound like tossing a shovel load of wet concrete into a wooden bin. He went back four steps and sat down heavily, making gagging noises and holding his belly. There was no more to do. I could have, and should have, stopped right there. But my throat ached and my left cheek bone felt like flame. I felt as swollen with anger as the hump of one of the black bulls of Miura. As the third man tried to run, I kicked his feet out from under him. He went down and scrambled up, turning, his face in silhouette against the car headlights. I caught him with one clean blow, an overhand right against the jaw shelf that sprung his mouth open and emptied his eyes and felt as though it drove my knuckles up into my wrist. I had sense enough to catch him as he toppled forward, or he would have smashed his face against the asphalt.

I got into my car. The southerner was stirring. Garson had labored up onto one knee.

"Stay away from my kid," he gasped. "You stay away from her."

I started the motor and drove away. I fingered my cheek bone. It was puffing, but it wasn't split. Each time I swallowed, my throat rasped with pain, but it seemed to be diminishing.

The Big Time Burger was ten minutes away. A white building set in a large lot. Spotlights were focused on a huge replica of a hamburger "all the way" that revolved slowly on a pedestal on the roof with the poisonous yellow of mustard, a sick red of tomato. The big lot was more than half full, the carhops busy. They wore tight, red, shiny, bullfighter pants, short white coats with gilt buttons, pert black hats with patent leather bills. There was a racked mike beside each parking space to use to place your order. Until the button was pressed on the mike it served as a speaker, rocking and rolling in a tin voice.

The girl who brought my beer was not at her best in skin-tight pants. She hooked the tray on the window, reached for my dollar.

"You know the Quarto boy?"

"Quarto?"

"He runs a yellow cut-down Ford with a fish-tail rear."

"Oh, those damn kids. They don't come to my station no more. They're over on the other side. Three hours of trouble and then a dime tip. Angie ought to run 'em off the place for good, but he's got no guts. One night some of them were busting bottles and Angie went out and they showed him a switch blade and he went and hid in the kitchen for an hour. They don't scare me. I just said, 'Kids, you eat at my station and keep stiffing me with them dime tips and maybe I can think up something real fancy to do to your food before you ever even get a look at it.' "

"I suppose the Paulson girl used to come here."

"Sure. She came a lot of times with that bunch that's over there now, and then a lot of times with college guys. Those college guys are fine. They want to look big so they tip as big as they can afford. Jane Ann Paulson, she was an okay kid. Never no trouble with her. And you know something? Lots of times that Landy came here. Once he parked right where you are right now, right in that beat-up Ford, and he had the other Paulson girl with him, the old maidy-acting one. I served them myself plenty of times. Always she didn't want nothing on her burger. Just plain. Her sister used to like them all the way. That was the car he used when he killed Jane Ann. He killed her because he wasn't getting any from the sister. It drove him off his head. The sister is a teaser. I think any girl does that is lower than dirt. I always say if you let a guy get all hot you got a kind of obligation to play along, don't you figure it that way?"

"Thanks a lot. When I'm ready for another beer—"

"Don't bother with the squawk box, mister. Just blink your lights and I'll bring the refill." She made change and I gave her a quarter extra and she thanked me and went away.

I got out and walked around to the other side of the building. There were about a dozen cars of noisy kids there. The noise had apparently driven the other trade away from their area. Their closely parked cars formed an island. Constant carhopping was going on. One young girl was doing a clumsily suggestive dance to the strains of rock and roll. She was barefooted and she danced on the roof of a sedan. A group of four boys clapped hands in time to the music. The rest of them were ignoring the girl.

I picked out the Quarto car and walked over to it. The top was down. There seemed to be ten kids in it.

"Ginny Garson here?"

"The man wants Garson." "Where's short, dark, and repulsive?" "Hey, Rook! Where'd your beast go? There's a suntan job wants a hack at the young stuff." "Hey, she's over with Smith, playing pooty-tat." "Mister Suntan, you see the showboat? The gray Cord with what Smith says is nine hand-rubbed coats of lacquer. Three over. Go look in the back seat. But knock first." "Knock and roll, Mister S.T." "Ole Smith'll come up with the hinkups if you interrupt his stuff. She's on loan-out from Rook. Hey, Rook?" "That merchandise is guaranteed. Never wears out. Don't you people ever finish a brew? I need a frail with a pail." I realized they were all half drunk. Long, golden girl-legs hung out in the chill October night. A half seen hand cupped a breast. They were half drunk and playful in the way that half grown lions can be playful. Rub them just a little bit the wrong way and they would have to find out if you had any chicken glands. They would cheerfully and efficiently cut you a little, or open the side of your face with a sharpened edge of a belt buckle. Or crush your groin with mail-order air force boots. While their women squealed because it was exciting. They were capable of forming a line-up on one of their own girls, or, with the callousness of the hen yard, pecking a weakened contemporary to death. They were revolt. They sheared off power poles and were found thirty feet from a tanned right arm with a homemade tattoo on the biceps. They died in flaming skids. There was nothing chicken about them. They had been informed about the world. They saw in the papers that everybody grabbed all they could. And there were slander-sheet magazines to tell them the inside dope on how their crooner heroes bounced from bed to bed. They knew the draft would catch them, that both parents and teachers had given up any last weak hope of discipline. Work was for the cubes—the quintessence of a square. The women were easy. There were always angles. They had it made.

And I could see how Nancy felt apart from this main stream, these social and emotional folkways of her contemporaries. Jane Ann had been a part of the group. Maybe she had been forced into it.

The Cord gleamed in the night. It was parked heading away from the lights, so the back seat was in darkness. I rapped on the roof of the car and asked for Ginny Garson. There was a slow stirring, a grunt of annoyance. The boy called Smith got out. He had a grotesque Mohican haircut, cold narrow Slavic eyes. He wore khakis and a maroon sweater with the sleeves cut off at the shoulder. His arms were long and heavily muscled, and he held his arms tensed and a little out from his body so the muscles would show.

"What's it about, friend?"

"I want to talk to Ginny for a few minutes."

"What's the rumble?"

The girl got out of the car. She wasn't tall. The sweater emphasized the ripeness and heaviness of her breasts. She wore tailored gray flannel slacks that went well with her yellow sweater. Her dark hair was worn in a mussy boyish cut. She looked up at me, her expression sulky, unpleasant, rebellious. She wore pale lipstick with heavy eye make-up. Except for her nose, her features were fairly good. An infatuated male might have thought the nose cute. It was small and pugged and tipped back so that her nostrils were too evident. It gave her something of the look of a pig.

"So what is it?"

"I want to talk to you alone for a few minutes."

"Say it in front of Smith."

"This isn't trouble, Ginny. I'm not law. It's a couple of questions. Let's say it's about where certain clothes came from. You remember who they belonged to, I guess. Now do you want to have a talk? My car's around on the other side."

"Clothes?" she said with exaggerated innocence. "What's with clothes?"

"Nobody wants them back. I just want to talk to you about them."

Smith put his arm around her. They stared at me with a hard and tolerant amusement. "You got a new way to get your kicks, chief?" Smith asked. "Go feel a woolly sweater. I know a guy goes for shoes. He's got a crate full of them."

I talked directly to Ginny, ignoring him. "There was money too. But they didn't find it until later."

I saw the quick gleam of interest in her eyes. She bit her underlip.

Smith tugged at her. "Honey, this type is a real conversationalist. Come on. Does talking send you any place?"

"Shut up a minute," she said. Smith let go of her and looked annoyed. "What are you after?" she asked me.

"Just some talk. I'm not law and I'm not a reporter. You don't have to pose on a tractor."

"Is there any money in this talk?"

"There could be, if it goes right."

"For God's sake," Smith said disgustedly.

"How much? I'm short this week."

"Twenty, if you really talk, Ginny. My car's around on the other side."

"You said that," Smith said.

She turned to him. "You mind too much, honey?"

He looked at her. He spat a casual six inches from my foot. "Take your time, baby. Take all the time there is. Take forever." He turned his back and headed toward another car.

"Darn it," Ginny said bitterly. "Well, let's get it over with."

We went around to my car. She wobbled and clenched her hips with each step, and kept her young breasts outthrust. I opened the door for her and she plumped in. I went around and got in beside her.

"Get me a Miller's," she said. "You owe me something."

I flicked the lights. The girl came out with the bottle. I ordered a Miller's. She peered in at Ginny, then gave me a look of scorn and disgust.

When the carhop walked away Ginny said, "So what about the clothes?"

"Jane Ann's."

"So she said if anything happened to her, I was to keep them. We both fit into them."

"Did she say anything was going to happen to her?"

She didn't answer until the waitress had left the beer and taken the money for it and walked away. Ginny didn't want the glass. Just the bottle. She tilted it up. "Let's get something straight. Nobody can prove she didn't say that, and nobody can

rove they ever were her clothes and besides, be-
ore I'd turn them over to that priss sister of hers,
'd cut 'em all up with a razor. So where are
ou?"

"You're a rough kid, Ginny."

"I get along fine. What's your angle? Want some
ut-up clothes?"

"You keep them, Ginny. Too bad you didn't have
. key to her locker. You could have cleaned that
ut too."

"Say, whatever happened to that stuff? I waited
or the sweaters to show up on Lady Iceberg, but
hey never did."

"Mr. Paulson gave them to the Salvation
Army."

"There's a type for you. That butcher. You know,
f my old man ever tried to bust me around the way
ie did Jane Ann, he'd wake up some morning with
. pair of air-conditioned tonsils. Every once in a
vhile I'd see the black and blues where he
humped her. I'd ask her why she took it. She said
t didn't bother her. She said she'd never let out
one yelp, and that always made him madder.
Look—whatever you're after, you better get to it. I
got to go group up again."

"Ginny, are you satisfied that Landy did it?"

"So that's it!"

"That's it."

"We've been kicking it around a lot. Rook says
hat Landy was too chicken. But everybody else
hinks it was his big brain. Like racing a motor
until you burn it out. His eyes were funny. Nobody
igures he was getting any kicks from Nancy.
Maybe sometimes she let him help her make fudge

or weed the flowers. But it's all just talk. I guess h‹
did it."

"But you have some reservations."

"It's been just dandy talking to you. It's been ‹
ball."

As she put her hand on the door handle and as ‹
opened my mouth to protest, a sedan turned int‹
the lot and a red dome light began to blink. Sh‹
tensed and watched it. It headed toward the othe‹
side of the lot. Car doors chunked and motors mad‹
raw sounds of power over the continuous music
Tires yelped. The cars scattered like a flock o‹
chickens when the hawk shadow moves across th‹
dooryard.

"Unhook the tray and set it on that shelf ther‹
and drive out slow," she ordered.

I did as she asked. She slid down onto the floo‹
and crouched half under the dash. A spotligh‹
caught the car, hesitated and then flicked away a‹
I drove out sedately and turned back toward town
She got back up onto the seat, drank the rest of he‹
beer, tossed the bottle into the ditch.

"Trouble?"

"That was Quillan. I don't dig it. He's village
It's the county cops make the most trouble. Peopl‹
report how Angie sells beer to minors."

"Why does he serve you?"

"Why? You got a ventilated head? Rook anc
Smith and Powie and the kids would tear his join‹
up for him. We tore up the Snack Shack one time
Rook had this hairy old jeep. We come out abou‹
four in the morning, hooked onto the roof anc
pulled it right off, honest. From then on we go‹

ervice, but nobody goes there any more. Don't ask
ne why."

"Where do you want to go?"

"Jeez, we didn't pick an assembly point, like we
lo when anybody's hot. We weren't figuring on
his. Go on back and park on the square and some-
ody will be coming by."

"You were saying you weren't completely cer-
ain that Landy killed her, Ginny."

"Was I saying that? I wouldn't say that."

"Who gave her the clothes, Ginny?"

"Probably her family."

"Come off it. You know what kind of clothes her
amily gave her."

"Then I don't know. She just had them. I don't
know where she got them."

I knew she was lying, and I had no real hope of
reaking her down. "Suppose we trade, Ginny."

"I don't get it."

"I'll tell you something you didn't know about
ner, and you tell me where the clothes came
rom."

"Why should I want to know anything about
ner? The kid's dead. She's been dead a long time."
She was elaborately casual. "Is it about money like
you said?"

"Well, you see what you think of this. While the
rial was on, her father found money hidden in her
room, fastened to the back of a dresser drawer. You
nad to take the drawer out to get to it. Over eight
nundred dollars, Ginny."

"Hey now!"

"And that's something you didn't know."

"Look, I knew she had some money. I don't know where she got it. She was all the time springing for the whole bunch. But I didn't know she had *that* much stashed. Wow!"

"So where did the clothes come from?"

"You already got the answer. She bought 'em. Usually I went with her. Sometimes we'd take the bus, but most of the time we'd get a ride over. We bought the stuff in Warrentown. See these here slacks? This is the best flannel you can buy. Forty-five I think these were. Somewhere around there. You know I felt kinda funny wearing her stuff, afterward. But they'd just go to waste. Now it doesn't bother me."

"She paid cash?"

"All the time. Better than half those sweaters were cashmere. And those add up."

"Park here?"

"Anywhere along here."

"You must have asked her where she was getting the money."

"I did. Mister, I asked her a hundred times. You can say we didn't have any secrets from each other. I knew that kid like I know myself. We did everything together. We compared notes on everything. If she had a boy that was real good, she'd hand him along to me and I'd do the same for her. But just that one thing I couldn't get out of her. Sometimes I'd get really sore. I thought for a while she was stealing from the market, maybe from the cash her old man brought home. She said she wasn't. She said the way he kept books, you couldn't even lift a Coke without he knew it. I finally stopped asking the one time she got real mad. She says to me,

'Damn you, Ginny. I get the money and we spend the money and you wear the stuff too. Isn't that enough? I got a place to get it. It's going to keep coming and there isn't ever going to be any trouble.' So I stopped asking. By then I guess I had it figured. Like this. She had some guy on the hook. I guess maybe she had the proof on him. Some family-type guy. Maybe some big church wheel. Jane Ann had a good head on her. She wouldn't try to bleed him dry. She'd try to just keep the money coming. Maybe fifty bucks a crack. And that would explain why she wouldn't tell me."

"Why not?"

"We were best friends like I said, but you should see how we live. I got two brothers in the Navy and they were smart to get the hell out. There's five younger than me, and my old man is just no damn good. I seen times there was nothing in that house but rice. The joint is ready to fall down. So what happens if she tells me? Sooner or later I go tap him too. And another thing, when I get loaded I tell every damn thing I know. Jane Ann could keep her mouth shut. Sooner or later I'd tell the kids and everybody would move in on him and spoil it quick. The one thing it did was give me an idea. I think I'm going to have me somebody on the hook. I'm playing him easy. Anyway, that's none of your damn business. I wonder where everybody got to."

"You don't know how she actually got the money. By that I mean how it was given to her. In person, or mailed to her, or left some place for her."

"I wondered about that. I know it wasn't mailed.

And I don't think it was a regular amount. Sometimes she was as broke as anybody. She hadn't been buying things for a few months before she was killed. I thought she was broke, but from what you say, she was stashing it. Say! I remember something. She hinted about maybe the two of us taking a trip. Nothing real definite, but I bet she was saving it for that. Jeez, it's too bad we never got to go. It would have been a ball."

"What did Jane Ann think of Landy?"

"She said he was certainly a good match for Nance. She used to drive him nuts trying to heat him up a little. She said she wished she could get him off some place and teach him some facts. But she wouldn't do it on account of Nancy."

"She thought that much of Nancy?"

"She wouldn't let us talk about what a cold fish Nancy is when she was around. She said if something was wrong with Nancy, there was one damn good reason for it. She used to try to make Nancy wake up and come alive, but it would just make Nancy cry. And she said that even if Landy was definitely on the creep side, it was good for Nancy to run around with a boy. I think Jane Ann was afraid Nancy would go queer. The only other boy friend Nancy had got drowned a little over two years ago. You know, it's funny. Jane Ann was younger, but she knew so much more that I think she felt toward Nancy more like I feel toward my little sisters."

"Do you want your little sisters to live just like you do?"

"Whip out your tambourine, brother, there'll be some holy rollin' tonight."

"I just wondered."

"Keep wondering. The Garson kids start with two outs and a full count and the bases loaded in the last half of the ninth, with Perry Score pitching. See what you think. What's the best angle? Sing in the choir and make yourself a virgin marriage to some clown who'll keep you swole up with kids for twenty years, or get out where the people are? Get out and sharpen up. Take your choice."

"Where are you going from here, Ginny?"

"Who wants to go? I'm already here. I'm having a ball. Maybe you ought to loosen up a little yourself. The way you rattle that tambourine gets on my nerves. Why don't you buy me a steak and then we can curl up some place with a bottle?"

"I guess not."

"How much is a dime worth? Eleven cents?"

"Not to me."

"You act it. I won't try to work you for more than the steak and the bottle."

"Jail bait, Ginny. Sorry."

"In this county? Sheriff Turnbull can't even spell statutory rape. Skip it anyway. I changed my mind. Who you working for?"

"Landy's sister. She isn't employing me. I'm a friend."

"That one. You know, Rook goes drooly over that one. He says she's a sex pot. That I can't make. To me all she needs is a broom and a pumpkin. Is she really any good? Rook is itching to know."

"I couldn't tell you."

"Why don't you just—Hey!" She reached over quickly and gave three fast taps on the horn ring. We were diagonally parked. The Cord eased in beside me, twin pipes burbling. Smith got out and came over to her side.

"Been cruising," he said.

"They want anybody?"

"I don't know. They blocked Quarto and gave him the strip job. Mickey, the damn fool, had two sticks on her. What was left from what Powie brought back last week. So real fast she eats them. So she's been heaving ever since. Quarto took her home. They didn't even lift Quarto's knife. He stuck it in his sock. It was a loose strip. Mickey could have stuck the sticks in her bra."

"It was better what she did."

"Maybe. You coming along?"

"Forever didn't last long."

"Come along or don't. It's Monday. Everything is breaking up. Maybe you should stay with buster here."

"It's a drag job. He says he's got better taste."

"Get out of the wagon, buster," he said.

"Me?" I said stupidly.

"Not too much, Smith. He's not a bad guy."

"Change your mind," I said. "This is something I'm getting sick of. If I get out of this car—if I'm forced to get out of this car, you're going to be a sick kid."

"This I eat," he said. He stuck his hand in her window and snapped his cigarette into my face. The sparks stung my cheek. The square was deserted. I got out. We met on the grass in front of the car. He feinted with his hands and kicked. I turned and took it on the thigh. He circled with hands held low, grinning. The girl got out of the car. In the silence I could hear her breathing louder than either of us. A street light made highlights on the rubbery ripple of his arm muscles. He was a quick and powerful kid. He moved well. I couldn't afford carelessness.

When he was close enough to warrant the gamble, I slapped at him with my open hand and my fingertips stung his nose. I saw the glisten as his eyes watered. "Get set," he said. "Watch this, baby."

She watched. He had a nice combination. He feinted a kick, hooked me hard under the heart and stabbed at my eyes with the spread, rigid fingers of his left hand. I had been waiting for that wrist. I snapped both hands onto it, turned to my right, turned his wrist so I could use the rigid arm as a lever. He clubbed me once in the back of the head with his right fist just as I got my shoulder neatly socketed in his armpit. I levered down and heaved. He went on up and over. I ended up on my knees, still holding onto his wrist. He slapped full length against the ground, and all the air went out of him in an explosive *whoof*. I climbed him, rolled him, levered his left arm up into his back, pressed firmly on the back of his head and ground his face into the grass. I stood up, hauled him to his feet, held the front of his belt and backhanded him across the mouth, then back again, forehand and backhand, until my hand stung and his mouth was raw. He was sobbing and he got his hand into his pocket. When it came out with the expected knife, I clubbed the nerve center in his shoulder and the knife fell. I spun him, held both wrists behind him and ran him headlong into one of the park elms, not too hard. He went down to his knees. I picked him up then by crotch and upper arm, took two half running steps and heaved him as hard as I could into a dense stand of lilacs. He disappeared entirely. I went back and picked up the knife. I stuck the blade into a crack in the curbing and snapped it off. I threw the hilt toward the lilacs. My thigh was tightening where he had kicked me. I massaged it with my knuckles. I walked back to where Ginny stood. I was show-off enough to make a great effort to keep my breathing normal.

"I remain uneaten," I said.

"Good God!" she said softly. "Did you—hurt him bad?"

"If he'd put up a fight, I might have. But he didn't."

"Smith can lick anybody in town but Barney Quillan."

"And me."

"Is he out? You know what he'll do? He'll wait and he'll come after you with a piece of chain."

I raised my voice so he could hear it. "He's not out. He's in there and he can hear us, but he's not moving. He comes out, and I'll throw him up into a tree. He's too ashamed to come out. He'd rather pretend to be unconscious and then he can be a big hero or something. I should have taken him over my knee. I forgot that part of it. And he won't come after me with any piece of chain because he has a hunch that if he does, he'll end up wearing it like a bow tie. He's a small town punk and from now on he'll move slow and easy with strangers. If he wants to stop me he's either got to get a lot of friends together or use a gun. And he better be a good shot. Ginny, you tell your pals how I used him like a wheelbarrow and ran him into a tree. He'll have a puffed mouth and a knot in his head and a shoulder that will stiffen up for a week. After that he can start parading his muscles again."

She moved closer to me. She looked up at me and licked her lower lip and said, "I'll come along with you. We don't need the steak or the bottle, do we?" She took my arm in both hands.

I got my arm loose. "That wasn't the idea. You stick around. Take care of him. He'll want to explain to you how it happened. Thanks for the information." I gave her the twenty.

She sighed. "Okay. So thanks for the beer, too. 'Night, now."

As I got in the car she walked toward the lilac bushes and I heard her say in a wheedling tone, "Okay, little bunny rabbit. You can come out now. It's safe. The bad man has gone away." As I drove around the square to park behind the Inn, I wondered if I had done some unknown stranger a large favor. Had my timing been a half second off, one eye might very well have run down my face. When I thought of that I wished I had thrown a real scare into him, perhaps sat on his chest and taken his knife and made him do some begging.

The police car was parked in front of the Inn. A big man was waiting for me in the front hallway. He sat on a small chair beside the breakfront that served as a reception desk. Charlie Staubs stood near by, leaning against a door frame, smoking a cigarette. Charlie gave me a quick warning look, a troubled look, and he shook his head slightly.

The man came up off the chair. You can tell a great deal about physical condition in the way a big man stands up. There was no puff of effort, no readjustment of weight, no positioning of feet, no thrust of hand to help him. He just came quickly and easily up onto his feet with the lightness of a puff of smoke. There have been men like him in all times and in all races. It is a physical type. Small, hard head fastened to broad shoulders by a neck as wide as the head. Heavy features, coarsened by the abuse of petty authority, eyes small under heavy tissue of brows, arms long and heavy, thick hands hanging half curled. A long torso and short legs.

He wore a gray corduroy sports jacket, a blue shirt open at the collar, dark trousers, black and white sports shoes. He could just as well have been wearing crude chain mail, and carrying the barbarian flail. Or the leather and short sword of a Roman legionnaire. There was a violence in him that excited the same apprehensive fear that you feel toward an uncaged animal.

"This is Mr. MacReedy," Charlie said. "Hugh—Barney Quillan."

He stood before me, legs planted, and studied me. He reached out very quickly and rapped a knuckle against the bruise on my left cheek bone. It hurt and I backed away and said, "What the hell!"

"You got a lot of trouble," he said. It was a deep rich voice with a liquid note in it, as though it bubbled up through dark oil.

"What kind of trouble?"

"We'll tell you all about it. We got a complaint from Garson. We got a lot of other things. You come along. Go ahead. Right out the front door."

"Anything I can do?" Charlie asked quickly.

"Get hold of John Tennant in Warrentown."

"That would be the one," Quillan said. "It figures."

I walked ahead of him. The inner door was open. He pushed me off balance as I tried to walk through it, and my shoulder struck the frame. "Drunk, too," he said.

I turned around, fists clenched. He stood, waiting for me, looking mildly amused and very dangerous. Behind him Charlie shook his head violently. I turned around again and went meekly out the door. I got into the car with him and he drove around the square and a half block off the square to a dark building I recognized as being the town hall. He drove around to the back. There was a light over the back door, two lighted office windows.

He pushed me in ahead of him, into the office. Just as I got inside the door he pushed me violently in the small of the back. I took two running steps forward and caught my balance by bracing my hands on the edge of a flat top desk. The man behind the desk was old and fat and pink. His fringe of hair was clean and white. His eyes were large, long lashed, of a vivid shade of violet. They were incongruous in the old pink face.

"Here he is and he's drunk," Quillan said.

"I'm not drunk."

"Sit down, please, sir," the man behind the desk said. His voice was high and merry, with a lilt of good cheer to it. "Sit down right there, sir. I am the Chief of Police here. My name is Score. Perry Score. Thank you, Barney. Suppose you have a seat too, and we'll go over this little matter. Jerry

Garson was very, very upset. One of his friends had to have a doctor, Mr. MacReedy. This is a small town. We deal very severely with violence of this sort."

"Three of them jumped me, as I was getting into my car."

"I assume you can prove the car isn't stolen. You have Chicago plates. Let me see your registration. Don't give me the wallet, please, sir. Just take the registration out and hand it to me. And your driver's license, if you will."

I realized as I handed the license over that it had expired and I had forgotten to renew it. The Chief pulled a pad over in front of him and wrote on it. He pushed the papers back to me. "So far, sir, you are accused of driving while intoxicated and of having an improper license to operate a motor vehicle."

"Just a moment."

"Let us get on, sir, to this matter of assault. Jerry Garson advises me that you pretended to be a magazine writer. He identifies you as the man who worked as an engineer on a construction job near here three years ago and who, at that time, was involved with the Landy woman."

"Yes, but—"

"When it was discovered you were lying, and that your purpose was to talk to Jerry Garson's daughter, the three men crossed the road with you, and they were remonstrating with you. You had learned where Miss Garson might be found. Without provocation, you attacked Jerry and his friends, injuring one of them seriously."

"That's a lie."

"It is up to the court to determine who is lying. Mr. Garson and his friends are willing to sign a complaint. We will drop that for a moment, sir. To continue, we have learned that you found Virginia Garson at a place called the Big Time Burger. You asked her to join you. She joined you in your car. You purchased alcoholic beverages for her. That can be construed as tampering with the morals of a minor, sir. The waitress will give evidence against you."

"But those kids were all drinking—"

"And when Quillan arrived in a police car, you left the area with the girl in your car."

"At her request."

"And, sir, you have contacted Miss Nancy Paulson and you have spent time with her. You were seen sitting on a bench together in the square. You helped the Landy woman move out of her apartment. You visited Landy in the death house. From your activities here, sir, it could be assumed that you are working as a private investigator. Do you have a license to operate in this state?"

"No. I—"

"If you had one it could be rescinded for your failure to inform police officials in the area of your operations. Operating without a license is a crime, Mr. MacReedy, sir."

"I'm just a friend."

"He asked Charlie Staubs to contact John Tennant for him, Perry," Quillan said.

The old man looked at me out of his incongruously beautiful eyes. He pursed eraser-red lips. "You felt you would have need of an attorney, sir?"

"Am I under arrest?"

"This is a small town. Up until this past year it was a very quiet small town, Mr. MacReedy, sir. We have had an unfortunate murder here. She was the daughter of one of the leading citizens of the village. Landy was a student in Sheridan College. The murder has complicated relationships between the town and the hill. We will all rest easier after Landy has been legally executed. It is my sworn duty to keep my neighbors from being annoyed by people like you, sir. I will not have you stirring up trouble. I will not have you blundering about in some amateur attempt at investigation of a crime that is already closed and off the books."

"Even if you didn't catch the right man?"

"That is an impertinent comment, sir. Lieutenant Frank Leader of the State Police conducted the investigation. The evidence was sufficient to indict Landy for murder. The jury found the evidence conclusive and brought in a verdict of guilty with no recommendation for mercy. The death sentence is mandatory, and has been passed. No further appeals are possible."

"Am I under arrest?"

"You know what charges we can place against you. You know that we can make some of them stick, sir. But it is an expense to the taxpayers to maintain you in prison. We would prefer that you check out of the Inn, get into your automobile and leave. Are you employed?"

"Yes. By Telboht Brothers, Chicago. I'm on a two-month vacation."

"The choice is up to you."

I looked over at Quillan. I looked back at the

Chief. I knew they could make a great deal of trouble. I hadn't handled myself very well. I couldn't see myself agreeing to leave and trying to sneak back into the village.

I tried to be ingratiating. Maybe that was a mistake too. "All right. I guess I've been out of line. You people probably have a legitimate beef. But I *was* jumped by those three men. I'm not drunk. I did buy the girl a beer. And now I'll give you something else. I had to rough up a kid. The others call him Smith. I parked and waited where the Garson girl told me to wait. Over on the other side of the square. He came along and snapped a cigarette into my face. I roughed him over and threw him into the bushes. I willingly admit that. And I admit that I've been trying to find out more about the murder of Jane Ann Paulson. There are three of us who are convinced he didn't do it. Victoria Landy, John Tennant and myself. And there are two who are half convinced he didn't. Nancy Paulson and Ginny Garson. I've uncovered something that didn't come out at the trial. It makes the case against Alister Landy look weaker."

Quillan gave a heavy snort of laughter. The Chief looked amused. "What is this evidence, Mr. Private Eye, sir?"

"Jane Ann had been getting money from somebody over a long period of time. She spent most of it on expensive clothes. She kept those clothes in her school locker and with Ginny Garson. At the time of her death she had over eight hundred dollars in her possession. It wasn't found until the trial was on and it wasn't reported. You could find the stores in Warrentown where she bought the stuff."

"I think you're making a mistake, sir. Speaking as man to man, we all know that Jane Ann was a wild kid. The village prefers to forget all that. If someone was giving her money, it has no bearing."

"Why not?"

"Let me tell him, Chief," Quillan said. "I had the Landy kid alone. I had him alone for three hours. I didn't leave a mark on him. Not one mark. And I got a confession. A nice juicy confession with all the details. But they didn't want to use it. Milligan figured he had enough. He figured the confession would be repudiated, see? And he was afraid Tennant would bring up how I got in a little trouble a couple of times, getting people to talk free like. So we know he confessed and plenty of people in this town know he confessed. So, like the Chief says, you still got your choice. Get the hell out, or get tossed in the can. And nobody is going to give you a hard time about the Smith kid, except maybe his old man."

"Hardesty Smith, Senior, is president of our bank here," the Chief said. "He suffered certain minor injuries—his son did—while resisting arrest by Quillan. I managed to save Quillan's job. We're still waiting, Mr. MacReedy, sir."

"I guess you better charge me, then. And get bail set."

Chief Score looked uncomfortable. "You aren't being reasonable. We're fair people here. We expect you to be reasonable. Mr. Quillan, do you think you could persuade Mr. MacReedy to be reasonable?"

Quillan got up. "Come on along, pal. Come with Barney."

When I tried to hold back, his big hand tightened on my arm. I looked back at the Chief. He looked flushed and pleased. He had a happy look of anticipation.

Quillan took me down a short hallway. "What are you going to do?"

"In here, pal." He pushed me into a dark room, turned on an overhead light. There was a table, a frayed couch, two sagging chairs, a single window. He spun me around and released me. "The Chief is a nice guy. Everybody likes the Chief. You don't like him."

"I don't like him or dislike him. I just don't want to be run out—"

He moved without warning, without any preliminary tensing of muscles. He thudded the heel of his hand against my forehead. It dazed me, and my neck creaked as I went back, stumbling against one of the chairs.

"That doesn't leave a mark," he said. "We aren't big time. But we don't leave marks. We're just village cops. We're easy to get along with. We keep a nice clean town here."

He moved slowly toward me as he spoke and I circled away from him. I wouldn't have felt safe with an ax in my hands. I wouldn't have felt safe with anything smaller than a Colt .45.

He grinned at me and said, "Now you're supposed to tell me what a big shot you are, and all about how I'm going to be in all kinds of trouble. Come on. Tell me." He blocked my way, moving me

back toward a corner. I sensed what he wanted. He
wanted me to fight back. I did a difficult thing. I
stood absolutely still, my arms at my sides, and let
him come up to me.

He moved slightly to the side and said, "Here's
another one." He swung and hit me across the di-
aphragm with the flat of his hand. It was like being slapped with a plank. I doubled over slightly
and he moved in front of me and snapped the cheek
bruise with a heavy finger. "You had that one
when you came in," he said. He then banged the
heel of his hand against my forehead. I hit the
wall, bounced off, fell to both knees. I stayed there.
He put a big foot against my chest and shoved. I hit
the wall again.

I knew then that it wasn't going to do any good.
Passive acceptance didn't slow him down. It made
it easier for him. I got up very slowly and as he
approached I started to turn away from him, and
then turned back, letting the anger flare up, using
the quickness and the violence that only anger can
give. I hooked him in the stomach with a left as
hard as I could. It was like hitting a padded tree. I
crossed the right to his jaw. He went back two
heavy steps. I repeated the combination and his
knees sagged. When I swung for his face the third
time, he pulled back away from the blow and hit
me, one thunderous right hand under the heart
that swept me off my feet. I came up as quickly as I
could, my whole left side knotted with pain. As I
tried to lead he caught my arm, pulled me half by
him, and chopped down on my left kidney with the
edge of his thick hand. I think I screamed. I twisted
loose. I knew I could not lift my left arm. Pain kept

it doubled against me. Everything in the room seemed to have misted out except his face. There was no expression there except a workmanlike concentration. I knew I had to hit him once more with my right hand, that I had to put everything into it and make the blow clean and certain. I swung and missed and he pushed me back as if I were a child.

"Wait a minute!" he said. His head was tilted. He was listening. He expected me to stop as though this were a kind of game we were playing. As I gathered myself to try again, he turned and opened the door and left the room. I staggered through the doorway, sick and dizzy. He walked to the entrance, massive against the light, seeming to fill the hall from side to side. I leaned against the wall, a great cramp in my left side, sucking air through clenched teeth. My vision was clearing slowly.

I saw him open the door, look down, lean over, pick someone up. The Chief came to the door of his office. I heard his shocked gasp. The two men went into his office. I saw one arm dangling, swinging loosely. The door was straight ahead. I shuffled toward it. I stopped when I came to the open office door I would have to pass, gathering my strength to move quickly.

I heard the Chief say, "I think it's the Garson girl. Good God!"

And instead of trying to make my run for it, I walked woodenly into the Chief's office. They had put her on a leather couch against the side wall. Quillan had lifted the phone. The Chief was bending over the couch. I moved close to him and looked down at her. Hard fists could have done that to her face. Hard fists or stones. One eye was swollen completely shut, the other nearly so. The tilted nose had been smashed utterly flat. The lips looked as though someone had gone over them with a wood rasp. One cheek was sickeningly indented where the cheek bone had given way. Her jaw sagged open at an unreal angle, and a sliver of bloody bone protruded through the flesh. Front teeth were broken off short. Her face and throat and clothing were torn and bloody. One heavy young breast was entirely exposed. Hands and knees were grimy. She had crawled a long way.

"Who did it?" the Chief was demanding insistently. "Who did this to you?"

She was breathing deeply, her breath wet and ragged in her throat. One hand stirred, and my stomach turned over as I saw a broken finger bent back at an impossible angle. The Chief must have realized as I did that she could not possibly speak. Her hand lifted. He scurried to the desk, came back with pad and pencil. He held it where she could see it, and he supported her hand.

She scrawled the name. "Smith."

Quillan came over. "The doc is on the way. She's hospital. He'll take her into Warrentown."

The Chief showed him the note. "Go get that kid."

"No kid, Chief. He hasn't been a kid for a long time."

"I don't care what the hell he is. Bring him in here. Maybe he's running. Give the license and the car description to the state boys."

Quillan made another phone call and left. I

heard his tires shriek and spin as he swung out. The Chief fussed over the girl. She lay slack, breathing and bleeding. I moved over and sat down cautiously. The sharpness of the pain was leaving, settling into a thick ache.

The doctor arrived. He was ridiculously young. The heavy, ragged artillery mustache did not serve its purpose. It made him look like a high school boy on Halloween. He gave me an absent nod and went directly to the girl, gently moving the Chief aside. From what I could see of his examination, he was quick and deft. He mopped up the blood, took a hypo from his bag, filled it, injected her in the upper arm. Her breathing changed quickly, becoming slower, deeper, more regular.

"I'll have to take her into Warrentown. She'll need X rays. I can't tell how badly she's hurt. There may be a skull fracture. Who is she and who did it?"

"Virginia Garson. Young Hardesty Smith did it."

He fingered her lips and said, "Can't use clamps here." He threaded a curved needle and began to sew her lips. "I'd say he knocked her down and then kicked her in the face repeatedly. Who brought her here?"

"She crawled, Don. Quillan heard her scratching on the door. He's got ears like a rabbit."

He nodded. He took gauze and bound up the sagging lower jaw. He examined her hand, fingering it lightly, and said, "Some small bones broken here. We'll save this for X ray." He turned toward me. "Please get the stretcher out of the back of my wagon."

I went out. It was a new station wagon with the seats folded down and a cot installed. I opened the tail gate and took out the rolled-up stretcher and took it in.

"Put it on the floor and we'll lift her down."

I unrolled the canvas stretcher on the floor beside the couch. Her face looked like nothing human. It was sexless, ageless, speaking only of violence. As the doctor reached for her shoulders she took a deeper breath and let it out slowly, shudderingly. He took her wrist quickly, fingers on her pulse. He dived for his bag, snapped it open, took out a hypodermic. She breathed that way again. For long desperate seconds she did not breathe at all. He injected her directly over the heart. There was one last thready, sighing wheeze and then silence. He worked over her for perhaps ten minutes while we stood and watched him. Then he straightened up slowly, took out a handkerchief and wiped his face.

"You'll want an autopsy," he said.

"What did she—die of?" Chief Score asked.

The young doctor shrugged. "Shock. Brain damage."

Chief Score sat down. "This is a terrible thing," he said. "These kids. I can't understand them."

The young doctor's voice was soft. "I've sewed up some ugly knife wounds. One kid got stabbed right in the corridor in the high school. They roar through the town without mufflers. I've tried to put them back together after the automobiles have ripped them apart. Teen-age girls expect me to be able to tell them where they can get a cut-rate abortion. They drink hard and they beat up strangers just for the kicks. People are getting tired of it, Chief. People are doing a lot of talking about it. The town is beginning to think you spend too much time shaking hands, and playing poker with Sheriff Turnbull. The parents can't control these kids. You could put the lid on. But it's too much trouble. You might make enemies, and then you couldn't deliver the vote for Turnbull. I think you and Quillan are a sorry excuse for a village police force, Chief."

"You have no call to talk to me like that, Don."

"The Landy case and now this. You're in trouble, Chief."

"Am I supposed to lock up every kid in town?"

The doctor stared at him. "No comment, Chief. Suppose you call the girl's folks. That'll give you something to do. I'll get hold of Hillman and have him send somebody for the body. Hooker can come over from Warrentown and do the autopsy over there."

He picked up his bag and left and we were alone with the body. The Chief picked up the pad and looked at it. He looked at me. "You were here. You heard me ask her. You saw her write it."

"I'll co-operate with you."

"You can go. Don't leave town."

"Am I under arrest?"

"Just go. Don't keep talking. Go."

I went out into the night. I was stiff and sore. I walked slowly back to the Inn. I felt that I was, in a sense, to blame. I had humiliated Smith. And, in memory, I heard her raw young voice, heavy with scorn, *Okay, little bunny rabbit. You can come out now. It's safe.*

So he had come out and kicked her to death.

Chapter 7

IT WAS MIDNIGHT ON MONDAY when I got back to the Inn for the second time. Charlie heard me come in and he came out to the front hallway in his shirt sleeves, inventory record in his hand, eyes wide with surprise.

"What are you doing loose?"

"Did you get hold of Tennant?"

"He said he'd be over in the morning."

"I better call him back."

"You move fragile-like, my friend."

"I had a little chat with Quillan."

"The decent people in this town would like to see him tossed out of here. Him and Perry Score. They run it like a little kingdom. When Score makes a mistake, he has the county backing him up. The county is in Sheriff Turnbull's pocket, and Turnbull is a white-haired boy to the big shots up at the capital. That Quillan is a sadistic son of a bitch."

"He showed me how he could do it without leaving a mark."

"We closed early downstairs. No business. But I can get to a bottle."

"That would help. You get it while I get hold of John Tennant. Then I've got a nice juicy story to tell you, Charlie."

Tennant didn't sound too annoyed to be disturbed again. I told him the additional facts I had learned from the Garson girl, and told him her guesses about Jane Ann's source of income. I told him about the shopping, and he said he would put an investigator on it in Warrentown. Then I told him of the death of the Garson girl, and of my part in it, and how it had saved me from a beating and gotten me released. He was shocked at the story, and said he knew Hardesty Smith, Senior, casually, and had the impression it was a good family. He said he would use the breathing space to send an investigator over to look into the Garson trouble, and it would not be difficult to prevent there being any formal complaint. And then he said something that turned my backbone to ice. He said, "Thinking it over, Hugh, it's damn fortunate the girl was able to implicate Smith. You might have had a very rough time."

I went into the lounge. Charlie was there with a bottle, glasses and ice. I made my drink. I told him what I had learned about Jane Ann Paulson, how I had learned it. I told him about the fight at the Garson place, about finding Ginny, about what she had told me. I told him about the scrap with Smith, how my little seance with Quillan had been interrupted, how the girl had scribbled the name and died there in Score's office.

"This is going to knock this town on its ear,

Hugh," he said. "The Smiths are prominent. Hardesty is a good man. He just couldn't handle the kid. That kid is no good."

"I thought he came from nothing. I thought he was all punk."

"You can't tell, these days. This is a terrible thing."

"But it gives me a breathing space. Score will need my evidence. He won't be riding me. All of a sudden I'm not as important on this other deal. In a way it's a break, but I'd just as soon not have had it this way. Not at her expense."

The drinks began to ease the aches and the tensions.

"What next?" Charlie asked.

"I'll go along with Ginny's guess. Jane Ann was blackmailing somebody. He is a man of a certain position in the community. Probably a wife and kids. At least a wife. He got out of line with her. She had some sort of proof. I would think she would have kept it with the money, if it was some sort of letter, but evidently she didn't. So I have to look for a man who hasn't been doing as well financially as he should have been doing. I don't think Jane Ann would have been stupid enough to be too greedy, but I'll bet she made the bite hurt. He had to be somebody she could contact easily and without anybody getting suspicious. He didn't mail the money to her. She had to make her demands known to him."

"And you think this man killed her?"

"I don't know. I have to find out. And it's the only lead. Now I'm too tired to think, and I'm half drunk. Can you think of a man who would match that description?"

"I'll think about it. I'll make a list. How about one of her teachers?"

"Could be. Could very well be. She could snatch his job right out from under him. Or it could be one of the professors up on the hill. She was headed up there the night she was killed, wasn't she? To see some girl friend?"

"That's right. Ann Sibley. Daughter of Dr. Wayne Sibley."

"Did she see that girl often?"

"I've got that impression."

I yawned and stretched until my shoulders creaked. I went woodenly up to bed. I tried to stay awake to think things through, but sleep came like a deep blue comber, the kind you can ride. Ginny's battered face floated through my dreams. In one dream it was Vicky who died there on the couch, before scribbling my name on the pad Score held for her. That one woke me up, sweaty and shaking.

I got down to breakfast at five minutes of ten, just under the wire. Charlie brought in a cup of coffee and sat down with me.

"They got the Smith kid. It was all on the eight o'clock news out of Warrentown. The state cops spotted him thirty miles north of here. They couldn't catch him. They radioed ahead. Another car blocked the road. He tried to take the ditch and flipped. It threw him clear. It banged him up pretty bad. He was still unconscious at the time of the broadcast. There was blood on his boots that they matched to the girl's blood."

"Is he going to live?"

"They think so. The Garson girl died of a brain hemorrhage. Everybody is going around shaking their heads and clucking. I'll bet they might just a well close the high school for all the work those kids'll do there today. It was the same way after Jane Ann's body was found, but this seems almost a little gaudier, if possible. There's talk of a Citizens' Council to take up the teen-age problem."

"Did I make the news?"

"They didn't say anything about that note. The way he ran for it is as good as a confession. I guess they think he'll confess when he regains consciousness. The newspaper people are over here from Warrentown already. Dalton is getting itself quite a reputation."

"Did you make up that list?"

"I tried. I can't. Hell, you know how small town businessmen are. Everybody talks poor mouth. That keeps them from getting hit too hard by the charities. They come out with big cars and when you admire the cars, they moan about the payments. How do you feel this morning?"

"Better than I should."

"You going to do anything about Quillan?"

"There's nothing I can prove."

"If I can get six or seven men together, will you tell them just what Quillan did and how Score asked him to do it?"

"If you think it will do any good."

"It may and it may not. I know the fellows I want to round up. I usually stay out of town politics. But I'm fed up with Score and Quillan."

After breakfast I drove to the motel. Vicky was out in the back garden in a sun suit. She wore dark glasses. She put her book down as I walked out. She seemed in fair spirits.

I told her everything that had happened. She asked questions and she looked so distressed when I started to tell her about Quillan that I made it sound as if I had gotten off a good deal easier than I had.

"I despise that man. I never told you what he did to Al. He had him there nearly a whole afternoon before he was taken over to Warrentown. Al didn't even want to tell me about it. I was there when he told John Tennant about it, when the question of the confession came up. Quillan made him sit in a chair. Quillan wrapped a Coke bottle in a towel. And he kept hitting Al over the head with it. Not hard, but continually. Each blow jarred his head. He said he got so he couldn't think or hear or see. And he knew the only way to stop it was to say yes. He didn't give any details of the crime. He didn't know any. He just kept saying yes while Quillan was asking the questions with all the details in them. Then they wrote it all out and Alister signed it. He had blinding headaches for three days, so bad that he couldn't sleep. And Quillan questioned me, too. He put his hands on me. Here. I told Lieutenant Leader and he made him stay away from me. They didn't try to use the confession. John Tennant said it would have been better for our side if they had because Quillan had made some errors in his reconstruction of the crime, and John Tennant could have proved they were impossible and invalidated the confession that way."

"Don't get so upset, honey."

"I get upset every time I think about him."

"Did you know Ginny Garson?"

"Just by sight. I'd seen her with Jane Ann. Al knows her better. Quite a few times he drove Jane Ann and Ginny over to the movies, as a favor. John Tennant pointed out that those trips could account for her hair being found in the car. But it didn't seem to help. They all seemed to have their minds all made up. They didn't seem to listen to John, no matter what he said."

"Can you think of any married man Jane Ann could have been blackmailing?"

"No. I've been wondering about that ever since you told me about the money. That's the way she would have had to get it."

"There's one boy who may be able to help. They call him Rook. I want to talk to him. And I want to talk to a professor named Sibley. I imagine you know him."

"Oh, I do. He's very nice. Dr. Wayne Sibley. He was very nice to me. He told me he had objected to my being released, but he hadn't been able to do anything about it."

I looked at her intently. "Is everything all right?"

Her mouth changed shape. "There's so little time, so very little time left."

"I'm doing all I can."

"I think you're doing a great deal, Hugh. I—I hope it's going to be enough."

"Ginny's testimony, if I could have persuaded her to give it, might have given us another stay of execution. It might have. There's no guarantee."

She took her dark glasses off, massaged tired eyes with thumb and forefinger. "This all seems like a strange dream, Hugh. None of it has seemed real. It couldn't have happened to us."

She looked small, forlorn and weary and my heart went out to her. Her hand reached out and tightened on my wrist and those so blue eyes looked directly into mine, almost blazing with intensity. "Don't let it happen to him, Hugh. Promise me you won't let it happen to him."

"I—"

"That was stupid of me. And unfair. You can't make a promise like that."

As I drove back to Dalton, the task she had set me seemed too impossible. Trained men had been over the ground. I had had a little bit of luck. The odds were that it was the last I would have. And that wasn't enough.

Professor Wayne Sibley had an eleven o'clock class. I waited on the second floor corridor of Delsey Hall outside the door of room 209. At five minutes of noon the classroom door opened and the students began coming out of that room and other rooms on the floor. A few of them gave me abrupt incurious glances. They seemed very young. Younger in some strange way than the kids in their chopped cars, the kids with their shrill girls at the drive-in.

Sibley came to the door and stood there chatting with two of the students while I waited over at the side. He was a stocky man with kinky gray hair, an outdoor complexion, tweedy clothes, a trained resonant voice. He talked amiably with the students, and they laughed at what he said. When they drifted off, he turned to me.

"Are you waiting to see me? I'm Wayne Sibley."

"Hugh MacReedy, Dr. Sibley. I'm a friend of Vicky Landy."

He studied me and I had the feeling he was making a decision about me. "I see. And you want to talk to me?"

"With your permission."

"Come along then. I have some papers to leave off at the administration building, and then we'll walk to my house. This is one of those blessed days without a one o'clock class."

"I—I certainly appreciate—"

"Don't look so startled, Mr. MacReedy. I'm willing to talk without putting up an argument."

"It isn't like the others I've tried to talk to, sir."

"I can imagine that. You stuck your jaw out when you proclaimed yourself a friend of Miss Landy. I also considered myself a friend of hers. But I have been a moral and social coward. And it has been on my conscience. As a friend I should have tried to help her. She is an exceptional young woman. I pride myself—or used to pride myself—on being a man of honor and integrity and courage. But this time the chips were down and I thought too long about the comfortable nest I've made for myself here, and I thought too long about what other people would think of me if I made a display of my friendship for her." He looked directly at me. "In other words, I have sickened myself, Mr. MacReedy. So I will talk to you without argument. And I hope you can think of something I can do to help her. Something rather difficult. Something that will make me so unpopular with my associates that it will serve as a form of self-punishment." He turned quickly away and I followed him.

As we cut across the campus I said, "Did you have Alister Landy in any of your classes?"

"For two years."

"What was your opinion of him, Dr. Sibley?"

"I prefer Mr. Sibley, Mr. MacReedy. I believe the title should be reserved for the more scientific degrees. I am an associate professor of English. I am also a victim of one of the more prevalent diseases of this age—parlor psychoanalysis. Alister Landy was one of the most intelligent students I have ever had. I could not like the boy. I was forced to respect him. His—intellectual arrogance was displeasing to me, even though I felt it justified. If you will forgive me for a moment, what proof have I that you are a friend of Miss Landy and not a journalist of some kind?"

"I—I guess the easiest way would be to phone Charlie Staubs at the Inn."

"My wife tells me incessantly that I am the world's most gullible man. I'll prove that by taking you at face value. Just a moment while I drop these off. I'll be right out."

He was out in far too short a time to have made a phone call.

"Can I drive you home?"

"I'd rather walk, thank you. It isn't far." I noticed that the students we met greeted him with what seemed to be a genuine fondness. "To get back to Alister, I believe I understood him. His parents died at the wrong time in his development. The experimental school he attended paid far too little attention to intellectual discipline. His sister, out of a sense of emotional duty, overprotected him. Too much of his thinking was intuitive. He would leap from peak to peak, unwilling to make the unexciting effort of plodding through the valleys in between. When I attempted to criticize his pattern of thought, I could not reach him. Brilliance, standing alone, is not enough. No one is too good for work. Things came far too easily to him. His memory was almost photographic. Isn't it odd how easy it is to speak of the boy in the past tense? Rather dreadful, I think."

"You think he commited the crime?"

"I've thought about it a great deal. I believe he did. The brilliant and erratic minds are so often not solidly anchored in reality, in the knowledge of the implacability of cause and effect. There is, of course, no such thing as an entirely normal man. It is trite to point out the correlation between brilliance and madness. And, after horror, the mind can provide its own anesthesia. I feel he was capable of doing that deed, doing it in such a dazed way that he committed innumerable errors, and wiping it out of his memory afterward. I would rather imagine that sort of mind is overly responsive to sex fantasy, to lurid imaginings. He turned fantasy into reality. The business of his emotional responsibility is something else again. He was declared sane. I cannot be that certain."

He walked with an even stride, staring at the walk ten feet ahead, frowning from time to time.

"You heard what happened last night."

"In the town. Yes. A horrible thing. But what can they expect?"

"What do you mean, sir?"

He shrugged. "It seems to me to be the result of a curious trend. A reversal of values. Basic decency is corny. Sex is used to sell refrigerators. Violence has become admirable. A boy is supposed to toughen himself, seek out the angles, display no emotion, disguise intelligence, avoid any stain of individuality. Public schools have become temporary stockades with such overcrowding that only the most devoted of teachers still try to stimulate intelligence and imagination. The welfare state guarantees that nobody will starve, no matter how badly they goof. And at the end you get your social security. So, from womb to tomb, you just let yourself sink into the warm selfish bath of conformity, of sex without emotional responsibility, of violence without punishment. Does this sound like a speech? I'm afraid it is. I've said it so many times I hardly need to pay attention any more."

"It's a black picture, Mr. Sibley."

"Not as black as I paint it, thank God. There's a new breed coming along. A batch of stern, almost painfully moral children, who have, through some miracle, become a bit sickened by their slightly elder contemporaries. The pendulum always swings." He turned in at a walk. "Here we are. Come on in, Mr. MacReedy."

The house was small, quite new, pleasant. He introduced me to Mrs. Sibley. She was a tall woman, almost too tall for him, with dark hair, lovely hollows in her cheeks, a look and air of gravity and composure that did not match a look of bright mischief in her eyes. In all, a most attractive woman.

"Mr. MacReedy is a friend of Vicky Landy," he said. "We have been talking about Alister. And soon, I imagine, he will want me to talk about Jane Ann Paulson. So, my dear, if you could join us on what we grandly call the patio, bearing three chill brews?"

She brought the beer out on a tray. The terrace was protected from the wind. It was almost hot there.

Sibley sipped his beer, set it down, put his fingertips together and frowned. "I make these assumptions, Mr. MacReedy. You are trying to help Miss Landy. The most help you could give her would be to discover, somehow, that her brother is innocent. I'm afraid that goal is unattainable. You have evidently been conducting your own investigation. Am I right?"

"Yes."

"In the course of which, you have learned, perhaps, many unsavory things about Jane Ann. And it puzzles you that she should have been a rather frequent visitor at the home of a college professor."

"That's right," I said, feeling uncomfortable at his intuitive accuracy.

"Lame ducks," Mrs. Sibley said.

"Precisely. That is a family expression, Mr. MacReedy. This family collects lame ducks. The emotionally halt and the emotionally blind. It is an affliction. We have learned to live with it."

"But this time there was more at stake," she said.

"This time the risk seemed not worth taking," Sibley said.

"Ann, our daughter," said Mrs. Sibley, "is emotionally quite mature for her age. She is honest and she is frank with us. I'm being objective. Otherwise we would not have taken that risk. As a member, so help me, of the P.T.A. in the village, I knew of Jane Ann's wildness and her reputation."

"Ann, I think, understood it before we did," Mr. Sibley said. "I guess you could call it a controlled schizophrenia. This is the home Jane Ann wished she had. We are the parents she wished she had. In some obscure way maybe she felt that had the coin fallen the other way, she could have been Ann. I am quite certain, and I know Ann wouldn't lie to me, that whenever Jane Ann came here, she was utterly different, not at all the way she was at school or with her friends. There was no contact between Ann and Jane Ann's friends, nor between Jane Ann and Ann's other friends. It was a curious relationship. Ann has told me that Jane Ann never talked of boys when they were together. It seemed necessary for her to be able to come here, and to have a normal uncomplicated relationship with another girl her age, uncomplicated by the tensions arising from the loose moral structure of her own group."

"When we feel we have anything to give to another human being, we like to give it," Mrs. Sibley said. "She seemed to gain something from coming here. We accepted her. She sensed that acceptance, and she needed it. We decided that there was no danger that she would try to corrupt Ann to her pattern. Had she tried that she would have destroyed this—this refuge."

"The fact she was headed here the night she was killed gave us some very unhappy publicity," Sibley said.

"And it was a very shocking thing for Ann," Mrs. Sibley said. "But I'm afraid that's rather a selfish viewpoint."

I knew that there was no lead here, not of the kind I had half hoped for. These people had far too much dignity and honesty, and the aura of love between them was apparent. I felt ashamed of my wild guess.

"Did you ever notice that Jane Ann always seemed to have money?"

"Yes. She bought Ann a wrist watch. A very good make and quite expensive. We would not let Ann accept it. Ann told us later that Jane Ann had given it to Ginny Garson. We had quite a job explaining to Ann just why she couldn't accept it," Mrs. Sibley said wryly.

"Do you think Ann would have any idea where the money came from?"

"If it came from where I think it may have come from, I hope Ann doesn't know," Mr. Sibley said.

"I have information which makes me believe that it came from one source, from one man. I think I'd like to know who he is."

Sibley looked at me and the corners of his mouth turned down in a savage little inverted smile. "And you thought it might be me?"

I felt my face grow hot. Mrs. Sibley giggled and then said, "Sorry, my dear. The vision was just too much for me."

"Let's not embarrass Mr. MacReedy. Seriously, I can see how it might be most interesting to find out who that man might be. I can't see any harm in asking Ann. Can you, dear?"

"I don't believe she'll know, but we could ask her. She got home five minutes before you did. They let the high school out today. I guess everybody was too upset or something. They called a teachers' meeting as an excuse."

She went and called her daughter. Ann came out onto the patio. She was not a pretty girl. She was blond, she did not have quite enough chin, and she was rather pallid; but her look was very direct, and her smile was warm.

"We've been talking about Jane Ann," Mr. Sibley said. "My dear, you remember we talked about Jane Ann being constantly in funds. Do you know where she got the money?"

"I—I don't really know."

"You sound uncertain."

"She wouldn't tell me. I asked her, but she wouldn't tell me. One day, it was a Saturday I remember, we went to the movies in the afternoon. We got out about four-thirty. We were hungry when we got out. We looked, but we only had about fourteen cents between us. Jane Ann said that didn't matter, she could get more. We went to the drugstore and she told me to wait right there in a booth for her. She was gone about five minutes. When she came back she had ten dollars. She showed it to me. I asked her who gave it to her and she said an old friend, but she made a kind of a face when she said it."

"Which way did she turn when she left the drugstore?"

"Right. I'm pretty sure."

"And she was gone five minutes?"

"It couldn't have been any more than that, maybe a little less."

"Did she have a bike?"

"No. We were walking."

"Do you think anybody could have given her a ride?"

"I wouldn't think so, Mr. MacReedy."

"Was there any other time when she got money like that?"

"N-No, but there was a time when she didn't. That sounds funny. It was another time we were in the drugstore. I think it was over a year ago. Last summer, I think. School wasn't on. There was a lipstick she wanted. She told me to wait. She came back and she was mad. She didn't have the money for it. She wasn't gone long at all. Maybe two or three minutes."

There was no other information. I thanked the Sibleys. They asked me to stay for lunch, but I refused. At the front door he told me he thought I was on a hopeless mission, but if I thought he could be of any further help, he'd be glad to talk to me again.

I drove down to the center of the village and parked on the square. I walked to the drugstore. It was on the west side of the square, four doors from the corner where College Street came into the square. I walked to the right, to the south. There were stores on either side of College Street, and others on the south side of the square. I estimated that I could walk to about fifteen places of business within two minutes. I felt almost certain she had gone to one of those places. It would be the easiest way in the world for her to get money. Suppose it were a candy store. She could go in and buy a dime's worth of candy. The amount of the purchase in itself could be a simple code. The proprietor, when he put the dime in the register, could put a ten-dollar bill in the sack with the candy. How he must have hated to see her come in, her face young and bland, her eyes greedy. He must have known that his only hope was to eliminate her. It would have taken a great deal of careful planning, of waiting, and of waiting for precisely the right chance.

Someone who could follow the movements of the Landy boy!

I stopped there in the sunlight, and conviction was so strong as to be an almost physical tug at the edge of my mind. I felt that if I moved carefully, and thought clearly, I could establish a connection. The proprietor of one of these shops would have had to be in a position where he could observe the habit patterns of Alister Landy. And he would have had to know that Alister and Nancy Paulson had quarreled. Otherwise Nancy would have provided an alibi for Alister.

Furthermore, he would have had to be close enough to some source of information to know that Alister was in the habit of taking night drives by himself, stopping nowhere. And he would have had to know that Alister sometimes parked with

Nancy in the obscure road by Three Sisters Creek.

The odds were that only one man who owned a business in this area could have been close enough to the girls, to the family, to the Landys, to learn all he would have to know in order to frame Alister Landy, and in that way get rid of the girl who was sucking him dry.

I walked again, slowly, and I looked at the store names. I stopped in front of a store. Mackin Hardware. And I remembered. Nancy had told me her family and the Mackins shared a camp at Morgan's Lake. Alister had been in Mackin's store before the murder. The knife had come from the store. Nancy had said the Mackins lived near them, at the corner of Oak and Venture.

A bell fastened to the back of the door tinkled as I walked in.

Chapter 8

MACKIN HARDWARE WAS REASONABLY MODERN, light, airy, and could have been very attractive. Gift items, such as electric clocks, toasters, bar equipment, charcoal grills, glassware, were in the front. Kitchen gadgets, pots and pans, knives and lighting fixtures were in the next segment. The rear of the store, in front of the glass-walled office, was taken up with tools, nails, paints, tubing, screening, plumbing and electrical parts.

Had the store been clean, the goods neatly racked, the floor swept, the slow-moving items dusted, it could have been attractive. But there was about it the subtle flavor of impending failure. There was a dusty smell, an air of negligence and slovenliness.

A woman came out of the back of the store and walked toward me. When she was quite distant, I thought she was an old woman. She moved with the careful fragility of age, and her heels scuffed the inlaid linoleum floor. When she came close I was shocked to see that she was not at all old. Perhaps not far into her thirties. It was difficult to tell. Her arms and throat were painfully thin, and you sensed at once that the watermelon bulge at her middle was not a pregnancy, but more likely a growth that was inevitably devouring her. Blond colorless hair was pulled tightly back. Her face was so shrunken that the pattern of the skull showed clearly. Her color was greenish paste, her gray eyes dulled. She pushed a wisp of hair back from her forehead with the back of her hand, and her voice seemed to come from a remote uncaring distance as she said, "Yes?"

"Do you have any—brass screws? Wood screws."

"Over here." I followed her. Her dress bagged on her wasted body. She indicated a shelf with a listless gesture of her hand. "What size?"

"Inch. Inch and a quarter."

She took down a small box. "Seventy cents. They run high."

I gave her a dollar and she shuffled toward the cash register in the middle of the store. I followed her. She put the box in a bag and rang up the sale. The drawer came open but she didn't reach in for my change. I looked at her. Her eyes squeezed shut. The arm of the hand that held my dollar was pressed against her middle.

"Are you all right?" I asked.

Her eyes opened slowly. She looked at me with what I imagine was supposed to be an apologetic smile. "Just a twinge. It comes every once in a while." She put the dollar in the drawer, gave me thirty cents and the paper bag.

"Maybe you ought to take some time off," I said.

"I only work when Billy can't make it. I'm Mrs Mackin. Part-time help is so hard to get. But I don't mind. It's this or sitting home. He's over to Warrentown today, to the bank."

"You have a nice store here."

She looked around, as though really seeing it for the first time, "I should do some sweeping. We don't get the trade we used to. They go over to the shopping center, a lot of them. You know how it goes. The trade drops off and then you don't order like you should and you don't have what the customers want and they go to the other places. Billy is seeing about a loan. I shouldn't talk about his business, I guess. But—you said it was a nice store. We own the building. We did a good trade in the old store. But that was before the shopping center. I ought to sweep the place up some." Again she closed her eyes tightly and I saw the cords of her throat jump into prominence.

"You should sit down, Mrs. Mackin. You're not well."

"This is a pretty good day," she said. "I felt pretty good the whole summer through. I sure dread the winter a-coming, though. It seems like spring never comes once the winter starts. The doctor, he's been giving me injections, ever since my operation. I'm coming along fine now. By next spring I'll be like I used to be, he says. Dr. Don Higel, his name is. He's kind of new here, but everybody says he's real good. Anything else you need, you come back."

"Thank you, Mrs. Mackin."

"You new in town?"

"Just visiting."

I was glad to get out. In addition to the smell of dust and hardware, there was a scent of illness in the close air, serious illness.

Quillan stopped me with a heavy hand on my shoulder just as I was opening my car door.

I moved clear of his hand and said, "What now?"

"Nothing special. Nothing special at all." He looked uncharacteristically unsure of himself. "No hard feelings," he said.

"What do you mean?"

He shrugged the massive shoulders. "I got a little excited. You know how it is. The Chief keeps pushing on me. I get a little worked up. No hard feelings."

"What's going on?"

His grin was heavy and unconvincing. He rubbed his jaw. "You got a good right hand. I guess you hurt me more'n I did you, huh?"

"Is this an apology?"

"You can call it that, I guess. Everybody makes a mistake sometimes."

"What are you driving at, Quillan? What do you want?"

"You know how talk goes around. Little town like this. I heard about some kind of committee. They want to talk to people. Maybe to you. You just say that everything was all right. We just asked you some questions. That's all."

"Is that young doctor on the committee?"

He looked at me blankly. "You mean Don Higel? I don't know. I don't think so."

"He had some strong opinions."

"He gets worked up. He doesn't mean anything. He can't do anything. You just say everything was all right if anybody asks you."

"Did Score tell you to talk to me?"

"I'm just talking man to man. Everybody makes a mistake."

"If anybody asks me, Quillan, I'll tell them you're right out of the dark ages, or the Hitler storm troopers. I'll tell them you belong in a slaughterhouse killing steers with a sledge. I'll tell them you're a sorry excuse for a town cop, a sadist, a bully, and very probably a psychopath. And I'll tell in detail how you worked me over at Score's request. That satisfy you?"

He stared at me. He glanced down the street. There were no pedestrians nearby. He jacked his knee into my groin. I fell back against my car, doubling over, grabbing the door handle to stay on my feet.

"That's for now," he said. "And I'm going to see if I can find you some place after dark, you smart son of a bitch." I heard the metal taps on his heels as he walked away. I managed to get the car door open. A woman pushing a carriage stared at me with disapproval. Drunk in the middle of the day. I fell in onto the seat, on the passenger side, too weak to reach the door. I was shuddering, and cold and sweaty. After a long time I was able to reach out and pull the car door shut. And a long time after that the pain had ebbed so that I could drive. I drove to the Inn. At the cost of considerable effort I was able to stand up straight enough to walk to my room without attracting attention. I rested on the bed, curled like a fetus, for nearly an hour. I undressed and took a hot shower. By the time I was dressed again, I felt almost normal.

Dr. Don Higel was able to see me at quarter of four, after a ten-minute wait.

He frowned for just a moment when I came in and then said, "Of course. You were in Score's office last night."

"Quillan was working me over when the girl came to the door on her hands and knees."

"What for?"

"I'm unpopular. I upset the two of them. I've been looking into the Landy case."

"That could make you unpopular. What seems to be your trouble? Quillan break anything?"

"Not yet. I want to ask you about one of your patients."

"I can't talk about my patients."

"I realize that. I have no official standing. I liked

what you said last night. I don't know that it will
do any harm to talk about this particular patient.
You can make your own decision, of course. I hope
you'll want to talk. It may have a bearing on other
things. Possibly an important bearing. Or I may be
way off line. I don't know. I think this woman is
dying. If I've ever seen death walking around,
she's it."

"I've got several who could qualify."

"Mrs. Billy Mackin."

He nodded. "Yes. Of course. Angela Mackin.
Farm stock. Tough as shoe leather. But not tough
enough to handle this."

"She's in the store today."

Higel looked distressed. He got up from his desk,
strolled to the window, fingered his preposterous
mustache. "I don't know where she finds the guts,"
he said softly.

"Did you operate?" I asked.

"I assisted. Seivers did it. Good man. Too far
gone, though. Took a look and closed her up."

"Does her husband know?"

"Yes. He's very upset about it. He blames himself. And well he might."

"What do you mean?"

He sat down at his desk and shrugged. "Take a
rational viewpoint. MacReedy—isn't that what
my nurse said?"

"That's right."

"Okay. You have a wife. Strapping wench. Full
of bounce. So she starts to slow down. Starts to lose
weight. Can't eat properly. Color gets bad. What
do you do?"

"Take her to a doctor."

"He stoked her with patent medicines. She was twenty-two pounds off her normal weight before I saw her."

"Could you tell me if she was home last April?"

He looked at me for a long time and seemed about to refuse. I think I saw a glimmer of some sort of comprehension in his eyes. He rang for the nurse and asked her to bring him the case folder on Angela Mackin. When the nurse brought it in, she gave me a curious look. She was a big-bodied redhead who looked as if she had been scrubbed with a wire brush.

He looked at the folder and closed it. "Operated on her on March eighteenth. Recovery was slow, if you want to call it recovery. Anyway she wasn't strong enough to come home until April twentieth. Frankly, I didn't expect her to get out of bed again. Amazing resistance. Tough."

"How much longer has she got?"

"She's overdue, MacReedy. I think now it will come fast. A month, probably less."

"Children?"

"One. It died in infancy."

"Is he a patient too?"

"No."

"But you know him?"

"Of course."

"Any general or specific opinions about him?"

"None in particular. I think you're asking too many questions."

"I'll change the subject. Do you think the town is about ready to get rid of Score and Quillan?"

"I certainly hope so. That affair last night was

sickening. I had a report from the hospital an hou
ago. The boy has regained consciousness. He con
fessed to beating the girl up, to kicking her. H
said he didn't mean to kill her. If the papers ar
smart, they'll play up just how it all started. At
drive-in beer joint which the county cops shoul
have kept in line. People are near the end of thei
patience. This may be the incident that does it
Turnbull is coming up for re-election. There's ope
gambling in this county. There is a narcotics prob
lem. It could be a clean county."

"I won't take up any more of your time. Thank
for answering the questions."

"If they're of any use to you, I'd like to know how
it comes out."

"If they are of any use, you'll hear, Doctor."

He hesitated, and then suddenly stuck his hand
out. I took it. There was a boyish grin half masked
by the bold raggedy mustache. It happens like that
sometimes. It is the way you find a friend, a good
one. And in all your life there can never be enough
of them. I understood him, bold mustache and all
A young and competent doctor in a small town. He
was too much man to restrict himself to the demands of his profession, arduous though they
might be. He could not accept the obvious flaws in
that environment. He could never help fighting for
what he felt was right.

From the way he had talked of Mrs. Billy Mackin I knew he was not the sort of doctor who ac-
cepts each case as a textbook problem. His patients
were human, and he was sensitized to humanity.
He would never achieve callousness, no matter
how long he practiced, no matter how gruff he be-

came. Dedication is rare, and when you meet it you can see the marks it leaves.

"Quillan gave you that contusion?"

"Not that one."

"You must be leading an interesting life, Mr. MacReedy."

"Maybe I'll get a chance to deal you in on some of the more interesting aspects, Doctor."

"Turn me into one of my own patients?"

"I hope not."

"There's been a lot of filth swept under a lot of rugs in this town. I see more than my share. I'll risk a laceration or two to throw back a couple of rugs. But don't ask me to talk about my patients, MacReedy."

"Hugh."

"All right. And Don to you, Hugh. You're digging into the Landy thing, you said. Isn't Mrs. Billy Mackin far afield?"

"I don't know. Maybe."

"They're both murder. But different in degree."

"Does talking about a dead patient violate ethics?"

"It might. I don't know why the hell I'm fencing, though."

"Remember Jane Ann's back injury?"

He stared at me in surprise. "You *do* get around." He sat down behind his desk. I sat down again. He loaded a pipe. It went appropriately and almost theatrically with his mustache. "Put me in a delicate position, that incident did, Hugh. I took over Dr. Kennedy's practice when he retired. I lost some people, of course. They thought I was too young. But I hoped to make it up on new residents. I had no intention of taking over any of Dr. Farbon's patients. I knew he was family doctor for the Paulsons. When Mr. Paulson phoned me and asked me to stop at the house I went to see Dr. Farbon. He filled me in. Paulson had been beating his daughter. She tried to wrench away and he hit her too high. With a piece of stove wood. Bruised the coccyx and tore some of the small muscles. Farbon knew he beat her, but he didn't know how violently. He hadn't had to treat her before. Paulson tried to lie about how it happened. When Farbon questioned the girl, he found out. He blew his top. He had delivered both those girls. You take an interest, you know. He blasted Paulson and Paulson ordered him out of the house. Though it's an account that pays on the dot, Farbon was glad to lose it. He's never liked Paulson. He told me to try to keep my mouth shut. I did. The girl was pretty bitter. The old man hadn't broken her spirit. He was practically arrogant about it. He was sorry he hurt her; but sorry only because he missed, not because he was beating her with a hunk of wood you could have felled a horse with."

"Would you call Paulson a psychopath, Don?"

"That's a handy all-inclusive word for the layman. He's a dour, humorless man, full of great pride, and very anxious to be a pillar of the community. I'd say he's a hypocrite and self-deluded sadist. He thought he was beating the girl for her own good. But I sense that it was a kind of release for him. He was beating an extension of himself, beating on the evil he sensed inside himself. His wife is spiritless, and the elder daughter won't sneeze without written permission from him. The typical autocrat. He couldn't break Jane Ann. In her own way she was as hard as he was. Maybe he toughened her into that hardness."

"But you get along with him?"

"I get along fine. I am the bright young doctor, competent and polite."

"Have any opinions about Nancy?"

"She's fouled up. Standard in that household, I'd say. Emotionally repressed. Scared of life."

I knew I had taken too much of his time. He walked me to the office door.

"Good hunting," he said.

"Thanks, Don."

"I know I don't have to tell you that anything I've said—"

"You don't have to tell me."

The redheaded nurse-receptionist smiled at me as I left. She told one of the patients to go in. I stood outside the small building and tried to make neat tabulations of everything I had learned. I could not make out mental lists. My mind doesn't work that way. I had met two good men. Higel and Sibley. But two good men were not enough to balance the scales against Quillan and Score.

The high school was not in session. I wanted to find a boy they called Rook. I hadn't seen the ones in Quarto's car distinctly, but I knew he was one of them. I cruised aimlessly until I saw a repair garage with some of the typical high school cars parked in the lot beside it. I parked and went in. Some of the kids were in there, working on a car.

"Can you fellows tell me where I can find a kid you call Rook?"

They looked at me with hostility. "He's all cracked up, man. That was his girl got stomped last night."

"I know that. What's his full name?"

"Evans is the last name. I don't know what the hell his first name is. It's one of those farms on the left on the Warrentown road. The name is on the mail box. Maybe two-three miles out."

I got to the farm at five. I parked beside the house. A big bald man in overalls came out of the barn and stared at me. He didn't come to find out what I wanted. He waited for me to come to him.

"Is your name Evans?"

"You read it on the box."

"Do you have a son the other kids call Rook?"

"Not in front of me, they don't. His name is Austin, after his mother's folks."

"Could I talk to him?"

"Why should you?"

"Why shouldn't I?"

He thought that over. "Are you a cop?"

"No. And I'm not from a newspaper. I talked to the Garson girl last night. I was trying to get some information from her. Your son might have that information. Its personal, and it's important to me."

"A reporter was out here this morning. That Garson girl was trash. He wasn't supposed to be seeing her. You can't keep them chained up. Running around, drinking beer, laying with trash. What can you do?"

"I don't know."

"I know what I'm doing. That kid is staying home. He isn't going any place. Not for a hell of a long time. That Smith was here sometimes. A bad kid. A mean kid, even if his people do have the bank. You look all right. His maw's down the road. You go there to the kitchen door. Go up the back stairs. He's in his room, moping and sniveling. First door on the left. Go talk to him if you want to."

He turned back into the barn. The house was very still. The back stairs creaked. The door was closed. I knocked.

"Who is it?"

"I want to talk to you."

"Who is it?"

I turned the knob. The door wasn't locked. The boy sat up on the bed. He wasn't a bad-looking boy, rangy and freckled. His eyes were red.

"I seen you," he said. "You were the one came looking for Ginny, then the cop car came and we lit out. Why did you turn her over to Smith, damn you?"

He looked at me indignantly. I turned a chair away from his desk and sat down and lit a cigarette. The pitch of the roof made the room an odd shape. There was a rag rug, quilted bed spread, battered maple furniture, pennants and pictures and traffic signs and rest room signs tacked to the flowered wallpaper.

"When I came along, Rook," I said gently, "it looked to me like you'd already turned her over to Smith."

He lay back on the pillow and looked at the ceiling, one long leg dangling, bare toes tapping the floor. "What can you do? She was crazy-acting. She did like she pleased. I knew her a long time. What can you do? Suppose I let it show what I felt like inside. Suppose I stop kidding around like I was. Suppose I want to make some kind of a big deal out of it. Then Smith bashes the hell out of me. She wanted to get in his car. Jeez, it wasn't my idea."

"So you let her go."

"Am I going to sit there with the guys and cry about it?"

"If that's the way she was, why do you feel bad?"

He came up onto one elbow. "You don't dig how things are. It isn't black and white. She was mixed up. It was that old man of hers. Way underneath she was a good kid."

"Way, way underneath."

"You want to make trouble? I'll give you trouble."

"Settle down. I roughed Smith up and threw him in the bushes. That was what made him mad enough to kick her to death."

He looked at me with new respect. "You're lying."

"Ask Quillan."

"I wouldn't go near Quillan." Suddenly his face seemed to crumple and he turned abruptly away.

"What's the matter?"

"I forget she's dead, and then it comes back on me. Hard."

"You knew her pretty well?"

"Sure. I wanted her to be different, I wanted her to be really steady. But it wasn't in her. I could get it, but so could a lot of other guys and I didn't like that."

"Just like Jane Ann?"

"Same deal. Only her old man was worse. He was worse than Jerry Garson."

"Jane Ann always had spending money."

"And she wasn't cheap with it, mister. She always treated. Ginny's got—Ginny had the clothes Jane Ann bought. Jane Ann could handle Smith. She used to make him beg. She laughed at him. She was the only one he couldn't scare. Wait until I get my hands on him. I'll take me a knife and I'll—"

"You'll have a long, long wait."

"I guess so."

"Did you know Jane Ann pretty well?"

He looked at me with cool suspicion. "Well enough. What's it to you?"

"Where'd she get her money?"

"Did she have any money? Did I say she had any money?"

"Come off it, Rook. This isn't a game."

"Then what is it? I don't know anything. Who the hell are you, anyway?"

"Ginny was trying to help me."

"Help you what? Did you take a piece before you give it to Smith?"

"Stop making it worse for yourself, Rook. I didn't touch her. She was a little girl going nowhere at all in a hell of a hurry, but she was willing to help me. She was willing to help me find out who killed Jane Ann."

"Landy killed her. Are you nuts?"

"I don't think so. If Ginny was willing to help, would you, for her sake, answer a question?"

He looked sulky. "I guess so."

"Do you know if Jane Ann ever hung around Mackin Hardware? If she went in there a lot?"

"That sounds like a stupid question."

"Maybe it is and maybe it isn't."

"Let me think. Jane Ann got killed a long time ago. Lots of things happen. It isn't easy to remember way back."

"Take your time."

He frowned, knuckling his chin, sitting on the edge of the bed. "I guess I remember."

"What?"

"Just seeing her going in there and coming out a lot of times. So what?"

"What would she buy in there?"

"What does anybody buy in a hardware store? Maybe nuts and bolts for her old man. Anyhow, those people, the Mackins and the Paulsons are real good friends. Maybe she just was stopping to say hello or something. They got the same place up at the lake. I saw it a couple of times, not during the season, when Ginny and Jane Ann and—" He stopped and flushed and said, "That doesn't matter."

"That's all you can remember?"

He stretched out again and looked at me, his face closed. "You're in my hair, mister. Why don't you go away? I don't want to talk to anybody today."

I knew I couldn't get any more out of him. I

didn't see anybody when I left. I wanted to go and see Vicky, but I didn't have enough to bring her. I didn't have enough to go on. I had told her not to expect me, that I wouldn't show up unless I had something concrete. And I didn't have enough to warrant contacting John Tennant.

While I ate in a diner, my first meal since breakfast—Quillan ruined any appetite I had for lunch—I thought over ways and means of getting to talk to Billy Mackin. I wanted to see him face to face. But I needed a good cover story.

After a lot of futile thought, I took my problem to Charlie Staubs. He was busy, but he was able to spare me a few minutes.

"So," he said, "you won't give me any reasons, but you want to talk to Billy."

"What kind of a guy is he?"

"He's all right. He's a good joe. Everybody likes him. He's having a bad time with Angela."

"I know."

"She was a damn fine-looking woman two and a half years ago."

"You'd never know it now."

"Hugh, are you going to get me in trouble?"

"I'm going to try not to."

Charlie sighed and tugged at his underlip and looked mournfully at the floor. He sighed again. "This is a small town."

"People keep telling me that."

"The odds are that he knows your name and knows you're doing some amateur investigating. Damn it. Say, I got an idea!" He hurried off. He came back in a few moments and handed me a business card. It said, *Walter L. Breckridge—Retail Properties.*

"What do I do with this?"

"Go over there and make like Breckridge. He stopped over here one night about a month ago. Comes from the West Coast. Billy won't know you by face."

"This could get me into trouble."

"Aren't you used to it?"

"What the hell do I say?"

"Ask him if he's interested in putting his store on the market. Make up the patter as you go along. He's not hard to talk to."

"I'll try it."

"If you've got any funny ideas about Billy, you better give them up."

The Mackin home was on the southwest corner of Venture and Oak, about a half block from the Paulson place. I judged that it would not be far from the back corner of the Mackin property to the back corner of Mrs. Hemsold's house where Alister and Vicky had lived.

The yard was scraggly, leaves unraked, hedge unclipped. It was getting dark and I saw a light go on in the house as I parked. I had the impression the house needed a coat of paint.

I stood on the shallow cement porch and rang the bell. Through the glass of the front door I could look down a narrow hallway to a kitchen at the end. A man got up and walked from the kitchen to the front door. He was silhouetted against the kitchen light. He was not a big man. The outside light clicked on. He opened the door.

"Mr. Mackin?"

"Yes?"

"Perhaps I should have phoned. I took a chance on finding you home. I'd like to talk to you for a few minutes?"

"Can you give me some idea of what it's about?"

"My name is Breckridge. Walter L. Breckridge. I deal in real estate. Here's my card, Mr. Mackin."

"I'm not interested in buying anything."

"You'll see by my card that I specialize in retail properties. I thought we might have a little talk about your store."

He nodded twice, stepped back and said, "Come in, please." His voice was amiable enough though colorless. "I'll have to ask you to talk quietly, Mr. Breckridge. My wife isn't well. I've just gotten her to bed. She had a bad spell a little while ago."

"I'm sorry to hear that."

He turned on a floor lamp. "You sit here. I left coffee on the stove. Can I bring you a drink? A beer, perhaps?"

"Thanks, yes."

When he came back and sat down opposite me, I had my first good look at him. He wore a blue dress shirt open at the throat, with the sleeves rolled halfway up his forearms. His hands and arms were heavy with black hair and they looked powerful. He had dark hair, a black Irish cast of feature, a blue beard-shadow on his jaws and throat. He moved trimly, confidently. His expression was alert and amiable, and the smile wrinkles in his face indicated that he smiled often and broadly. He looked somewhat tired. The room we were in was too full of overstuffed furniture, too cluttered with lamps, knickknacks, figurines. There were gilt-framed mirrors on the walls, a copy of the "Blue Boy," a copy of Stuart's "Washington." There were souvenir pillows on the couch.

"Have you taken a look at the store?"

"I was in there today."

He frowned. "Temporary help is almost impossible to get. Angela said she felt able to take care of it today. I guess it was too much for her. I shouldn't have let her do it. I had to go over to Warrentown on business. I told her not to try to clean up, and I know it needed it."

"You don't seem to have a great deal of stock, Mr. Mackin."

"There's more than it looks like. I guarantee that. I could give you the exact inventory figure, but the books are down there. Somewhere around twenty-one thousand. And I own that building. Syler's, the other store in the building, leases from me. I've got a good, steady business there. A good, loyal trade. I don't know as I would be very interested in selling."

"Then I guess I'm wasting your time, Mr. Mackin."

He leaned forward and lowered his voice. "I don't want to inflict my personal problems on you, Mr. Breckridge. I'll be frank with you. My wife doesn't know it, but she hasn't long to live. And when she—has passed away, I don't know if I'll have the heart to continue here. We've had—eleven very happy years together." His voice broke and he leaned back and covered his eyes with his hand.

"I'm terribly sorry."

"I assure you that under any other circumstances, I wouldn't think of selling out. It will just mean making a fresh start. But—the pleasure has gone out of it."

He uncovered his eyes and looked at me quite appealingly.

"Do you have a client who is interested?" he asked.

"A man who might be interested. I can't divulge his name at this time. He's not a local man, of course."

"Of course."

"We investigate very carefully before we contact the owner."

"You do?" He looked slightly distressed.

"I understand your volume of business has fallen off. The shopping center on the Warrentown road has apparently hurt your trade."

He smiled sadly. "It's my own neglect that's hurt it. You can understand how I have—let things slip. But it would take a very short time to get back to the gross I was doing before."

"I don't want to offend you, but we have been led to believe that you are in personal financial difficulties."

"Completely wrong!" he said sharply, and then lowered his voice. "I own that building, as I told you. And I own this house. I can tell you, though it's none of your business, that I have practically no cash reserve. Illness is expensive, Mr. Breckridge."

"There is another property in this town my client is interested in."

Mackin looked alarmed. "There is?"

"Paulson's Market."

He leaned back and grinned at me. It was a very charming grin, impudent and conspiratorial. "Dick will never sell."

"You know him that well?"

"He's been like a brother to me. An older brother. I know him like this." He twined first and second finger. "Do you know, when I came to this town, I rented a room in his home. That was thirteen years ago. His girls were tiny then. He helped me get started in business. Why, we own a camp together, at Morgan's Lake. It's like we all belonged to the same family. Myra has been like a mother to Angela. And I can assure you that Dick will never sell out. That store is his life. If he had been willing to sell, he would have sold at the time of the tragedy."

"Tragedy?" He stared at me so sharply I saw that I had made a mistake. "Oh, of course. That was stupid of me. It was his daughter, wasn't it, who—"

"Jane Ann Paulson was raped and murdered by a pervert, a college student named Landy. It was in every paper in the country. It isn't the sort of thing you forget. She was a lovely girl in every respect."

"Of course. I had a temporary lapse of memory."

"They electrocute the fiend next Monday."

"There seems to be a lot of violence in this town. My client—"

"You mean that business last night. Hardly typical. It won't happen again in twenty years. Let's get back to business. You say you've investigated? What tentative valuation have you put on the business? Remember, the stock I have is quality stock. It moves fast."

"We'd prefer to have you name a figure."

"If I were to sell, and I'm not certain I will, I think I would have to have around a hundred and ten thousand. That includes land, building, stock and good will."

"What is your equity in the building?"

"That isn't pertinent, is it?"

"It might be. How about the Syler lease?"

"It has nine years to run at a hundred a month. There's better than ten thousand right there."

"Less upkeep, repairs, taxes, water, light and—"

"They pay their own utilities."

I sipped my beer. He was willing to wait me out. He sat, apparently relaxed, but I sensed tension in him.

"Would you say Mr. Paulson would be easy to talk to?"

"Hardly. I'm probably one of the few people he can relax with. He's a very proud man, and a very stern man. He has very fixed ideas of right and wrong. He wouldn't like it if he knew you were asking about him."

"But he took you into his home."

"I'll be grateful to him all my life. He knows that. I even met Angela through them."

"Do they know how ill she is?"

"Is that just idle curiosity?"

"I'm sorry. I'm wondering if he'd be hurt should you sell out and move away."

"I said nothing about moving away. I believe I'd stay here."

"What would you do?"

"Work for someone for a time. Maybe even Dick. Give up all responsibilities. Try to forget. I was eighteen when he took me in. I'm thirty-one now. Did you see Angela when you went to the store?" I nodded. "She's only twenty-nine. That seems incredible, doesn't it?"

"It certainly does."

"I blame myself. I should have been more careful of her. Her mother died of the same thing. We waited too long. She doesn't know it, of course. She thinks she's getting better."

He covered his eyes with his right hand again. This time it had a more phony flavor than before. He was a very plausible man. He was a very controlled man. And, to make Paulson like him and relax with him, he had to be a very clever man. With his eyes covered, I could see only the lower half of his face in the slant of the lamplight. His mouth was heavy and sensuous. The left hand, resting on the chair arm, was as heavily haired as the paw of an animal. It seemed a mistake for him to cover those plausible eyes with the grin wrinkles around them.

"I suppose you wouldn't want to leave because you have so many friends here, Mr. Mackin."

"It a good town. People are nice here. I never really had a home before." He lowered his hand and gave me a sheepish smile. "I guess you could say I was a bum. Dick put out a helping hand.

There isn't anything I wouldn't do for him."

I stood up. "Thanks for the information. I'll pass it along. You'll hear from me."

"May I have your business address, please?"

"I'll get in touch with you, Mr. Mackin."

His eyes looked narrower. "I'm afraid I'll have to have your address. I have to know who I'm doing business with." He was standing up also, and I noticed that he had managed to drift toward the doorway without seeming to move. He wasn't big, but he was deep-chested, with broad shoulders, and he was quick. There was a quality of menace about him that I hadn't sensed before, a menace utterly unlike that exuded by Quillan. This was the tension of the stalking cat.

"I'll write it on the back of the card I gave you."

He took it from his shirt pocket and handed it to me. I wrote an address on the back. I wrote a Chicago address, the address of the home offices of the Telboht Brothers Construction Company, with the digits of the street number scrambled.

"It seems like a long way to come for the kind of commission you'd get."

"The client is an old friend. We don't expect to make money."

"Why not put him in touch with a reliable firm in Warrentown?"

"We suggested that. He wanted us to handle it for him."

"He must be a very good friend."

"He is."

I was glad to get out into the night, away from the smell of illness, away from the wiry plausible man with the grin wrinkles that had begun to me to look as though they had been cut there for the purpose of deception.

I drove a block in the car and parked where there were no lights. I leaned back and tried to reconstruct it. The young daughter of a close friend. Maybe one summer day they had been left alone in the cabin at the lake. Maybe she had come into the store just at closing time. There were any number of ways it could have happened. And I could see him succumbing to that particular kind of weakness. There was about him a flavor of virility—but not the masculine virility of man, or bull, or ram like the virility of a Quillan. His seemed a more sly and insinuating breed—the virility of a cat or serpent. The eyes smiled too readily. The little touching gestures of grief were a bit too carefully posed.

I had everything, and yet I had nothing.

I felt certain it was Mackin. I tried to doubt my own certainty and I could not. Yet if there was one outstanding element of his mind, it was the element of calculation and control. He would not be caught off guard. He had very nearly caught me off guard. I didn't know if I'd satisfied his innate skepticism with the invented address. If I hadn't, he would check it. If he did, he would be more than ever on guard. And he could be dangerous.

Jane Ann had been able to handle him, to use him to her own advantage. I wondered if she had really sensed the danger in doing that. He was a proud man, with a capacity for violence.

I went back to the Inn after a time and went to bed. I could not sleep. I wanted to place a trap for him. I could think of no trap subtle enough yet effective enough. I did not doubt but what he had murdered his wife. He had murdered her through purposeful negligence, just as surely as if he told her to walk across a mine field. She still breathed, and slept and had pain; but she was dead.

Paulson had taken him in. He had put him on his feet. Billy Mackin was thought to be a successful businessman, worried to distraction about his sick wife. "A good joe," Charlie had called him. I could see Mackin at a village picnic, wandering around with that engaging grin, saying the right things to everyone. He was the lizard which could change its color and blend with any environment. What man was he? The proprietor of the hardware store? The canny bargainer? Or was the real Mackin the man who held the knife and pursued the screaming girl through the alders?

He could slap a back and tell a funny story. He would be the youthful gallant with elderly ladies. He would be a reliable baby-sitter in emergencies. I sensed that there were so many facets to the man that there was no real substance. If there was any area in which a man like that might lose control, it was the area of the sensual, the quick black demands of the wiry body which, in need, would choose not a partner but rather a victim. And I had seen the outward evidence of vanity, the glossy black of the hair combed thickly and carefully back over small well-set ears, the hand-sewn seams of the expensive shoes on the neat narrow feet.

Mackin was close to the Paulsons—close enough so he would know Alister's habits, know of the quarrel. Angela Mackin had been in the hospital the night of the killing. An April evening, when it would have been perfectly normal to roam around the back yards of the section where the Mackins and the Paulsons and the Landys lived.

He could have seen Jane Ann start out. He would have known where she was headed. He could have seen Alister Landy start out in the Ford. From then on it was simple. Follow quickly. Pick Jane Ann up on the hill. Take her far beyond the college, off to the obscure road where the college kids parked, where perhaps he had followed Alister and Nancy. Rape and murder in blindness and in fury and in revenge for all the requests. Another fifty dollars. Another forty. Sixty more, please. Or I'll tell.

Tell what?

It didn't seem to dovetail neatly enough. Tell what? What could he lose by denying it, telling her to go ahead and tell. If there was proof, where did it go?

I tossed and turned and thought and finally slept.

Chapter 9

TOWARD MORNING I must have slept very deeply, because I awoke and could not remember for long seconds where I was. Then I heard the wood mill whistle, heard traffic around the square, saw the Williamsburg blue of the bedroom walls, and had the feeling of coming back into myself, a return of the spirit after long night journeys.

This was Wednesday, and there were five days left, and what I could see of the sky looked gray. I thought of the boy in the cage who could see no sky, only the impersonal fluorescence. He would hear the muffled sounds of the awakening of the prison, hear the slap of ace on jack in the endless card game, the clank and thud of bolt and door as his breakfast was brought.

I hoped Vicky still slept, and that there was more comfort for her in sleep than in wakefulness. Jane Ann slept deep under the October grasses, with gray wind moving unheard through the drying leaves that still clung to cemetery elms. And Ginny, her best friend, slept now, perhaps more restlessly, in the closed coffin at Hillman's Funeral Home on Vineland Avenue. Perhaps through the years of infinity, those two could complain to each other in bodiless voices of how short life had been, of how small a share each had been given.

And in the house at the corner of Venture and Oak, Angela Mackin would be asleep, the defeated body fighting against invasion, lungs wheezing a staleness, blood moving slowly to nourish the rebel cells. Billy Mackin would be near her, and he would count the slow breathing, and make computation of how many exhalations were left. At twenty-five a minute, at fifteen hundred an hour, at thirty-six thousand a day, those lungs would move one million more times.

Somehow I could not imagine Mackin asleep. I

could see him feigning sleep, as though he were some invader from an alien planet forced to conform to our needs to prevent suspicion. I could not imagine him asleep, or as a child, or weeping.

I wondered if I was being too imaginative about him, because it did not seem possible to me that he could have lived here for so long without others being aware of a curious aura of evil about him, a special calculated alertness. In all honesty I knew that I looked at him and saw what I wanted to see. It was the same way that others had looked at Alister Landy and seen, in his every gesture and change of expression, the pervert, the rapist, the murderer. Suspicion creates a wrong interpretation of each symbol. It may well be that there is a blackness in each one of us that, on an almost primal level, responds to the darkness in another—sees it and understands our kinship with every foulness—just as we have an equivalent kinship with every grace. Direct public suspicion at any honest man, back it up with a distortion of facts, spread new slanders; and not only will there be a quick willingness to believe, but the man himself, made aware of all this, will give all the responses of guilt as he tries to persuade all of his innocence. The blush of outrage is no different in tint than the blush of shame.

I could think of no trap for him. I could think of no way to find proof. An expert accountant might be able to go over his books and find that there had been a constant drain of money that had ceased with the death of Jane Ann. Yet Mackin had only to confess to an imaginary infatuation with an unknown woman, or to a weakness for dice. It could be proven that Jane Ann had funds from some unknown source. It could be shown that Mackin had the opportunity and the necessary knowledge of the movements of the principals to commit the crime successfully. But that was not enough. There had to be more.

And I had a feeling that there was more information that I did not have. The crime seemed unnecessarily involved, more complicated than the circumstances demanded. I felt as though I could see only a portion of Mackin's motivation.

I dressed and went down to breakfast. When I was nearly finished, Mary Staubs came in and told me that a man named Arma wanted to talk to me. He was waiting in the lounge. She had told him I was having breakfast.

Arma was a dark, serious young man, compact, rather pallid though husky-looking, icily polite. He showed me credentials. They identified him as Lawrence T. Arma of the Bureau of Criminal Investigation of the State Police. We sat in a corner of the lounge, near the front windows. He had a stenographer's notebook. He explained that he worked with Lieutenant Frank Leader in a special section that did homicide investigation for the state prosecutor in those areas where municipal police forces were not equipped to handle such investigations. He said that he had worked with Lieutenant Leader on the Landy case and that now he was after information on the Garson case. Chief Score had told him that I could give evidence.

He wanted my full name, occupation, permanent address, birth place, date of birth. He printed proper names in his notebook and took the rest of the information in fast competent-looking shorthand.

"Now just tell me what happened Monday night."

"Where do I start?"

"You were with Miss Garson, I understand."

"Not exactly. I wanted to talk to her."

"You knew her? You had dated her before?"

"Look, Arma. Let's get on the right track. I'd never seen the girl before. I have no intention of dating any jail bait."

Some of the icy politeness vanished, and he looked more human. "Sorry, What did you want to talk to her about?"

"Didn't Score tell you that? She was Jane Ann Paulson's best friend. You must have known that."

"Yes. We talked to her in the spring. What's your interest in the Landy case?"

"I—I intend to marry Victoria Landy. She isn't convinced her brother did it. Neither am I. That's a very unpopular attitude around this town."

"I can see how it would be. Why did you want to talk to Ginny Garson?"

I told him about the money, the clothes, the shopping trips. I told him of Ginny's speculation about where Jane Ann was getting the money. I did not tell him my suspicion of Mackin.

"Why are you taking this down?" I asked him.

"Mr. MacReedy, I can't afford to have any opinion of the Landy case. It's out of our hands. We can't reinvestigate. You picked up something we missed. I can see how you fell over the information, but that isn't an excuse for our missing it. I can see why the Garson girl wouldn't volunteer information. She wanted to keep the clothes. I can take this all down because it has a very indirect bearing on the Garson murder."

"Do you people have any official objection to my nosing around?"

"You have that right. Just so long as you don't claim to be an officer of the law, carry a gun, or bully other citizens, or take pay for your work."

"Are you satisfied with the Landy conviction?"

"Lieutenant Leader is satisfied. It was a good piece of work."

"Can I ask you one question about that? It's something that has been bothering me."

"Go ahead."

"There was so much physical evidence against Landy that I have to go on the assumption he was framed, and the evidence planted. The tire track can be explained by the fact he and Nancy Paulson parked there the previous night. The hair can be explained by the fact that Jane Ann had ridden in the car on several occasions. The blood, the knife and the purse would have to be the objects planted. But there was a chance they would never be found. That would endanger the actual murderer. I would think that after going to that trouble, the murderer would have done something to direct suspicion on Landy, rather than just wait and hope you fellows would be sharp enough to locate that evidence."

Arma looked troubled. He made an aimless doodle in the margin of his notes. He didn't answer.

"I've talked to John Tennant," I said. "Suppose

there had been such a signpost pointing at Landy. That would increase any amount of reasonable doubt that he had been framed. Tennant would certainly have brought that out at the trial. It might have helped."

"I'm not in any position to tell you anything."

"But you know something. Maybe with what I have and what you have, Tennant could get another stay of execution."

"I don't have anything that would do you any good."

"You aren't a lawyer."

"But I know the rules of evidence." He sat for a time, apparently making up his mind. He sighed heavily. "So okay. So I stick my neck out. I've got to trust you not to make a big stink about this. If you try, it'll be denied by Leader and by everybody else. By God, I'll deny it too. I'm only telling you because maybe it will help a little, give you a little more to go on. It bothered me at the time. It still bothers me. Every time you get a case like that one, you get a lot of tips, many of them anonymous, usually all of them worthless.

"Get the picture, now. Frank was going ahead on his project, checking every car that any college kid had access to. We set up our field headquarters at the town hall. The town was crawling with reporters, cops and cranks. We'd imported lab people and set up a makeshift lab. They were clearing the cars as fast as they could. We had to get one all the way back from Alabama. A kid had flunked out and driven home between the time of the murder and when the body was found. If I remember, this incident happened on Friday afternoon. Frank and

I walked out to the car we were using. As we got in, I saw something on the floor. I picked it up and looked at it. It was a three by five file card, unruled. Somebody had cut out newsprint and pasted it on the card. Just the name Landy. Separate letters, different type sizes. I gave it to Frank. He looked at it and grunted and stuck it in his pocket. I asked him if we should turn it over to the lab and he said it didn't mean anything. When we got back I checked the master list they were working on. I saw that one student named Landy had access to a car. They hadn't gotten to it yet. They got to it that same day. I don't know if Frank moved it up on the list or not."

"Isn't there a law about suppressing evidence?"

"Look. I work for the guy. He's a sound officer. He's a plodder. He likes leg work. He likes it the hard way. And he's ambitious. It looks a hell of a lot better if he finds Landy his way than if he follows up a tip. I never saw the card again."

"Did you think it was important?"

"I thought it could be."

"Why?"

"Because it was a way of giving us a tip with an absolute minimum of risk. The chance of tracing it would be just about nothing. The lab could find out what paper had been used, what kind of glue, what make of card. And run into a big dead end. Whoever tossed it into the car, if they'd gone to all that trouble, certainly did it without being observed. Maybe he carried it around for days before he had the right chance. It was safer than a phone call, a hell of a lot safer than a letter. Another thing. In a crime like that, feeling was running so high that anybody who could have given an accurate tip would have been a hero for a day. The care used was, to me, suspicious. It had a smell of guilty knowledge."

"After you found out it was Landy's car, did you talk to Leader about it?"

"I tried to. At first he said he couldn't remember it. I described it to him. He said he had thrown it away and it was probably the work of some crank. A lucky guess."

"Tennant could certainly have used it at the trial."

"After Leader talked to Landy, he was certain in his mind that the kid did it. He likes first degree convictions. They look good on the record."

"I think I should tell Tennant about this."

"Go ahead. And tell him I'll deny it."

"Suppose he tries to drag Leader into it?"

"He won't. He knows Frank."

"Was it common knowledge then that you were going over the cars, one by one?"

"No. Not then. Not when that note was left in our car. Later on people knew because it was too big to keep secret."

"So whoever put the card in your car had no way of knowing you would eventually get to Landy's car?"

"No way. That's right." He sighed. "Now I've got something else to worry about. Let's get back to business. You went looking for the Garson girl."

I told him about going to the house, about being recognized, about the fight. After the fight, Garson had reported it to Score, and Quillan had come out to the drive-in to intercept me. I told him about driving away with Ginny and parking at the square, how she signaled to Smith, about the fight with him. I went into complete detail about all contact with Quillan, about how Ginny wrote the name on the pad.

"Did she seem to be aware of what she was being asked? Could she have just written his name because she wanted to see him?"

"I can't tell you that. There wasn't enough face left so you could tell her expression. I think she heard Chief Score. The town hall is about two hundred yards from where he must have beaten her up."

"We found the place. She walked part of the way, crawled the rest."

"If she could do that, I think she could hear what he said. You have a confession, don't you?"

"Here's where reasonable doubt comes in. Maybe he knocked her around and drove off. Then maybe somebody else put on the finishing touches. It isn't likely, but a doubt can be created. This one can't be made first degree. And probably the lawyers will be too smart to let it come to trial. With those damn, black, bloody boots in evidence, a jury would be too big a risk. Trial is only mandatory in first degree. If his old man can swing enough weight, it may end up with him copping a plea of manslaughter and drawing five and serving three. That would be the very least. Ten years on the inside is more likely. I've seen him. No matter how long a time they keep him in, he's going to be bad news when he gets out. Congenital psychopath. They can crop up in anybody's family."

"What about Quillan?"

"What about him?"

"What do you think of his methods?"

"Stupid. He can go just so far. Then somebody slaps him with a criminal suit and a civil suit, sends him to the can and strips him of anything he happens to own. In the line of local cops, a town usually gets just what it deserves."

I told him about the daylight attack on the street, and about Quillan's threat. He took it down and said, "Here's what you do. If he jumps you, go to a good doctor. Get a detailed report. Contact me. I'll turn it over to the right people. It may take some time, but they'll fix him. I can use the transcript of this as evidence."

"Do I have to sign your transcripts?"

"Yes. I'll bring them to you or have them brought to you. Probably tomorrow."

We stood up and shook hands. As soon as he had left, I phoned Tennant and said I wanted to see him. He said he could see me in his office at eleven-thirty. I was five minutes ahead of time, and the girl told me to go right in. It was an old-fashioned office on the third floor corner of a red brick building. The windows looked out over the busiest corner in the small city. Tennant sat behind a disorderly desk piled high with papers. He grinned at me and waved me to a chair close beside the desk. He had a round thing in his hand, one of those puzzles with a glass cover and steel balls that have to be rolled through a maze to a center point.

"This is my thinking machine," he said. "The cigarette break used to stimulate the little gray cells, then I gave up smoking."

"I thought you were smoking the other day."

"I gave up office smoking. I frown with great rectitude at visitors' cigars. All week end I am a furnace. What have you got that you couldn't give me over the phone?"

I told him Arma's story about the tip. He kept rolling the balls in the puzzle, but I knew he was listening with great intentness. When I had gotten part way into it he interrupted me, opened a cabinet door, turned on a tape recorder, put the mike on the littered desk and asked me to start over. When I had finished he asked me a few questions, mostly about Arma's attitude. He turned the recorder off, got up, and paced around, hands deep in his pockets.

"I know Larry Arma," he said finally. "He's careful. This isn't like him."

"Maybe he's got a guilty feeling about Alister."

"More than that. He's pretty cold. He keeps his guard up. I think it's a calculated risk. He wouldn't have done it two years ago. Now he's in pretty solid. He was recently promoted. He's ambitious. I think he thinks he's big enough to take a chop at Leader. He knew damn well this wouldn't stay bottled up. And if he's forced to make a statement, he'll do so. With great reluctance, of course. I'll bet he was looking for a good place to drop that information. The knife will go in so easily, Leader won't even feel it. It's a break for us. A very tiny one, but a break. I have to play it just right to get anything out of it. And still we may get nothing."

"What do you mean?"

"If I broke it now, Leader would deny it. Maybe

Arma would too. It all dissolves and they burn the boy on schedule. So I have to wait. I wait until Sunday night. Then I phone the Governor, and I say that I have evidence that the State Police suppressed evidence in the Landy case that tended to show the innocence of my client. If my timing is right, and my voice is right, and I hint that I'm giving it to the papers along with the fact that I have talked to him, he won't know what I've got, how flimsy it is. Maybe he'll grant another stay. That gives us a little time. Then we work on Arma. And if we can get co-operation from him, which is still dubious, I might be able to wangle a retrial. It's worth a chance."

He sat down again and looked at me. "And what else have you been doing for amusement, Hugh? Looks like you got nudged in the face."

I told him.

Then, picking the words with great care, I said, "I believe that the man who killed her is named William Mackin. He is a neighbor. He runs a hardware store. His wife is dying. He and Paulson are joint owners of a camp at Morgan's Lake. He's close to the family. I believe he is the man Jane Ann was blackmailing. But I can't think of any conceivable way of proving it."

He waited for perhaps five seconds. "You've talked to this man?"

I told him of my masquerade. He winced a little.

"You are positive?"

"More positive than I should be. I realize that. I haven't got enough to go on to be this positive."

"I have a great respect for hunches, Hugh. Intution, whatever you want to call it. The subconscious mind is always at work, sorting, filing, rejecting. Then something floats up into the conscious mind. You don't know where it came from. That doesn't make the groundwork done by the subconscious any less valid. I'd think that you must have other reasons for being so certain of Mackin. Perhaps things you heard and placed no conscious valuation on. Maybe you've collected more evidence than you're aware of."

"I can't think of what it could be."

"Is he well liked?"

"He seems to be."

"And that knife came from his store. Wait a minute! I know the man. I have a memory like a sieve. Milligan called him as a prosecution witness, to prove Landy had been in the store on Thursday, the day before the crime. And Milligan introduced photographs of the inside of the store to show that the open display of the kitchen knives could not be seen from the street or from the office in the back of the store. I did a brief cross-examination. I remember him well. He seemed plausible, concerned. Seemed to me like a solid citizen. And not the kind you can mix up on cross-examination."

"Why did Alister go into the store?"

"He went that time to get some paint. He was a fairly frequent customer. The apartment in the Hemsold house was in bad shape and the landlady was pretty stingy about maintenance. Al and Vicky tried to keep ahead of the slow rot."

"You saw him then, and you remember him. Do you think he'd be capable of a thing like that?"

"That's a naïve question. I've been around th
law too many years to try to make that kind of
guess. The best man on homicide here in the War
rentown force looks like a congenital murderer
The most vicious crime I ever heard about wa
committed by a charming boy who looked as if h
could be the captain of the Dartmouth ski team
Every face is a mask, Hugh."

I spread my hands helplessly. "I think he's th
one. What do I do next?"

"Nothing juvenile, like twisting his arm. You
were juvenile enough posing as a real estate man
He's had a lot of time. And he looks like a man wh
can think clearly. He won't have any evidenc
around. He doesn't look like the type who can b
trapped or intimidated."

"So?"

"Let me make an assumption. It's based on m
experience and on my reading. It is a very seldor
thing for a man to go up and commit a rape murde
out of the blue. The knife wounds were clear evi
dence of the extent of aberration. There is, in al
most every case, a long history of lesser acts. Peep
ing, exposure, all the way down to the furtiv
pinch in the crowded elevator. It is a sex obsessior
and there should be evidence of it in his pas
life."

"But maybe he just wanted it to look like—tha
kind of a crime?"

"Very improbable, Hugh. A normal murderer—
and there's a hell of a strange phrase—would fin
it impossible to go through with that sort of thing
I think we better put some people on him, and fas
And I'll tell you this. If we pick up just one littl

indication that Mackin has committed abnormal acts, I'll join your one-man parade, beating a drum."

"Do you think I could tell Vicky about the Frank Leader thing?"

"I wouldn't. It's too likely to fail. I'm sorry. I have to run. Lunch date."

"What shall I do?"

He grinned at me. "Just keep blundering and stumbling around, Hugh. You have a great talent for doing the wrong thing at the wrong time in the wrong way, and coming up with a right answer."

After I had lunch on the outskirts of Warrentown, I took another road that brought me out near Vicky's motel without having to go through Dalton. She was not there but her car was, so I checked a restaurant and found her in the first one. I had coffee there with her but we could not talk because the other tables were too close. She said she felt restless, so we went for a drive in the wagon and talked as we drove.

I told her my suspicions of Billy Mackin. At first she seemed to feel I was too far out in left field. But I built it for her, adding everything but the card flipped into Leader's car. I told her of my talk with Arma and with John Tennant.

She said, "I don't know Mr. Mackin well. He's waited on me several times. His wife's waited on me too. I used to go to their old store when we first came to town. She's changed horribly since then. He seemed—nice enough, I guess."

"A fragment of doubt?"

"It isn't anything unusual. Whenever he was there, he would wait on me. With a sort of insinuating manner. There's an old fashioned word for it. A masher. He's really quite an attractive man. But that sort of thing happens to any presentable girl in any number of stores. It doesn't signify."

"Did you like him?"

"Well enough, I guess. At arm's length. I never thought about liking him or disliking him."

"Did you ever hear any talk about him? The kind of talk that John Tennant is trying to uncover."

"No, but you know I never did get very close to the townspeople. My friends were all up on the hill. I'm sorry, Hugh. This just doesn't seem real to me. I can't make it seem real. He's close to the Paulsons. Jane Ann could have gotten money from him. He could have seen Jane Ann start out, and he could have known Al would be alone in the car. He could easily have known about my date in Warrentown. Then killed Jane Ann, rubbed bloody clothing on the seat of the Ford, buried the knife and purse in the flower bed. But it's all so devious, so darn complicated. That keeps it from being real. He had a motive for killing Jane Ann, you say. All right. But why go to such dangerous lengths to make it look as if Al did it? He had nothing against Al. I don't see how he could have."

"I know what you mean."

"All this ought to cheer me up. It doesn't."

"I'll have to take you back, Vicky. I want to go back to Dalton and poke around a little and see if I can pick up any kind of gossip about him."

"I remember hearing one thing about him that

was said sort of in a mean way. I forget who said it. The money for the store, they said, was from her. After her people died, she got the money from the sale of the farm."

"Every kind of information we can get will help."

I left her at the door and drove to Dalton. I drove as fast as I dared and managed to get to the high school at two-thirty, just as the kids were getting out. I parked where I had before, and when Nancy Paulson went by I saw her mouth tighten. It was a look of displeasure and it made me doubt that I would see her in the park. Nevertheless, I drove down and parked and found the same bench empty. The afternoon was getting colder. There was a thin smell of winter in the air. The wind had taken so many leaves in the last two days that the square was beginning to have a bare look.

Forty minutes later, as I was beginning to give up hope, I saw her coming. She wore slacks and a short coat. She sat tentatively on the far end of the bench and gave me a cold glare. "I shouldn't have come. Somebody told my father they saw me talking to you. He wanted to know about you. I had to lie to him. It makes me feel sick when I have to lie to him."

"What did you tell him?"

"I said you were one of the new teachers this semester and I just stopped and talked. He thought that was all right."

"But you came back anyway."

"I won't talk to you again. This is the last time. I came to tell you that. So there's no use of you parking again like you did. I won't come here."

"Will you talk now?"

"Not for long."

"You must have known Ginny Garson."

"I don't go around with that crowd."

"Didn't you say she was your sister's best friend?"

"No. Ann Sibley was Jane Ann's best friend. Ann is nice. Ginny was a bad influence on Jane Ann." I could see by the primness of her expression, the tilt of her averted face, that it was pointless to try to remind her of the things she had told me before. She had slipped away from me. Her voice was lighter, more childish.

"Do you feel sorry about what happened to Ginny?"

"I don't know. Maybe. It was a terrible thing, I guess. But like I said, I didn't know her hardly."

I could well understand Alister's frequent impatience with her. This was the immature mind in action. I wondered if he had sensed the true depth of her sexual fears. I despaired of getting very far with her. I had somehow lost her co-operation. Yet I had to find out if she had any pertinent information about Billy Mackin.

"Your family and the Mackins are very close, aren't they?"

She turned her head and stared at me, apparently confused by the change of pace. "Oh, yes," she said. "He lived in our house when we were little. We own a camp together. He is my father's very best friend in all the world." The last sentence had a curious sing-song intonation as though it had been memorized. She stared right at me, which was unusual for her. Usually she would meet my gaze with quick, flickering little glances. Her eyes were wide and solemn and without guile. For a moment I could not recall what that look reminded me of, and then I remembered. In Panama I had a house boy who was a paragon of cleanliness and honesty with but one exception. He dipped into every opened bottle of liquor and every opened carton of cigarettes. When accused he would look at me in exactly the same way. It was the overly bland look of guilt, of the uncomfortable lie. But this could not be a lie. Richard Paulson and Bill Mackin *were* close friends.

She looked away. I was troubled. I did not know how to pursue the subject further.

"Why did you look at me like that, Nancy?"

"Like what? I don't know what you mean."

"Billy Mackin is your father's best friend. Did Jane Ann like him?"

She turned again toward me, far too bland and honest and convincing. "Jane Ann liked Billy very much. I like him too. He is a wonderful man. He is my father's best friend."

"You're looking at me that way again."

She flushed with both confusion and anger. "I just don't know what you're talking about. Or why you're talking about Uncle Billy."

"Is that what you call him?"

"We used to call him that. Now we—I—call him Billy on account of he said he liked it better."

I could think of only one possibility that might account for her curious reaction. Suppose that family tradition required her to feel fond of Billy Mackin. Yet she despised him. She was cowed by her father. She could force herself to believe, on the surface of her mind, that she liked Billy. Then the subconscious pressure of her hatred for him would give her that too bland look of the unpracticed liar. And it would bring that sing-song quality into her voice, that flavor of childish chant.

"And you like him too?"

"Of course I like him. He has always been good to us. I don't know why you keep asking me about him. He is my father's very best friend and he lived with us when we were little."

I could see no way to penetrate the wall. And I knew it was a wall. I sensed it had been built up over a long period of time. I wished I could remove one stone and look on the other side of that wall.

"Has Billy Mackin ever given you money?"

"Yes, and other things too. Presents on my birthday and Christmas. We give him presents too. And Angela."

"Angela is very sick, isn't she?"

"Yes. And Billy is very upset. She's been sick a long time. They say she is going to die." Her manner was more that of eleven than eighteen.

"Did Jane Ann ever go in Billy's store?"

"Yes. We both went to Billy's store. Lots of times."

I leaned slightly toward the look of wide-eyed innocence. "Do you go there at all now?"

"No," she whispered, and she had a look as though a shadow had moved behind her eyes, drifted quickly across her conscious mind.

"Why not?" I asked sharply.

"I do go there. To buy things. Yes, I go there." There was a shrillness in her voice.

"Then why did you say you didn't?"

"I didn't say that. You—you're getting me all mixed up. I don't know what you—"

"You're mixed up, Nancy. But I didn't mix you up. You're mixed up all the way."

"I'm not. I'm not!"

"Then why should you be starting to cry? I'm only asking you about your father's best friend. You ought to be able to talk about Billy Mackin without getting all mixed up."

"But you—"

I leaned closer, and made my voice harsh. I punished her with my voice. "I'm not mixing you up. You can answer simple questions. Why do you hate Billy Mackin? What happened to make you hate him?"

"He is my father's—"

"—very best friend. And you hate his guts. Why?"

I don't know what I expected. I wasn't prepared for what happened. Her face and body went rigid. Her eyes focused beyond me for a moment and then rolled up until I could see but thin slices of the bottom of the irises. Her jaw locked and the muscles at the corners of her jaw bulged against the skin. Her hands had been resting on her thighs. The fingers curled back, almost impossibly far back. Cords in her neck stood out. Her breathing was fast and shallow and very noisy.

"Nancy!" I said. There was no change. I put my hand on her shoulder to shake her. Her shoulder should have been soft. It was like stone. I was frightened. It looked like some sort of fit. Her color was very bad.

I heard footsteps approaching rapidly. I turned and saw Mr. Paulson hurrying toward us. He had put a coat on. He hadn't buttoned it. The white butcher apron showed where the coat was parted. His face was ghastly white, mouth so bloodlessly tight it was like a half-healed scar. The wind had disarranged the careful camouflage of hair over the bald head. Billy Mackin was twenty feet behind him, hurrying along in a gray topcoat, gray felt hat with small green feather in the band.

"Nancy!" Paulson roared. She started to come out of it even before he grabbed her arm and yanked her to her feet. She looked dazed, as though coming out of deep sleep, looked around as though to orient herself. He pushed her with a vicious explosion of strength. She stumbled and very nearly fell. "Get on home. I'll tend to you later, young lady."

She walked slowly away, not looking back. Her walk was somnambulistic.

I had stood up. The bench was behind me. Paulson and Mackin faced me, side by side.

"Why are you bothering my daughter?" Paulson yelled into my face.

Chapter 10

PAULSON WAS A BIG MAN, and so angry that he shook, and his voice shook. Mackin looked scornfully amused. There wasn't a soul within sixty feet of us.

"I told you, Dick," Billy Mackin said. "A meddler. I thought there was something funny about him. I described him to Perry Score. He's a pal of the Landys."

"What did you want with my daughter? She lied to me. She said you were a teacher."

"I was asking her some questions about Jane Ann."

"What is your name?"

"His name is MacReedy, Dick. He's staying at the Inn. He's the one who was hanging around the Garson girl before the Smith kid killed her. He's the one who beat up on Garson and the Smith kid."

"What are you doing here?" he demanded.

"Let me answer him one time, Mackin," I said. "I'm here to prove Alister Landy innocent."

He stared at me as though I'd lost my mind. "Innocent?"

"Why not? Other innocent people have been convicted. Not often, but it happens."

"It didn't this time."

"Why argue with him, Dick?" Billy said. "It isn't hard to figure. He's trying to stir up trouble enough so maybe that shyster Tennant can get another stay of execution. That will put MacReedy here in big with Vicky Landy. What the hell did you come around and bother me with a bunch of lies for, MacReedy? You make a lousy real estate agent."

I looked at him as steadily as I could. "I wanted to find out what kind of a man you are."

He grinned at me. It wasn't pleasant, but it was certainly disarming. The hint of the feline behind the grin was very remote. "Trying to elect a suspect, maybe? You must be hard up. Now ask me where I was at the time the crime was committed."

"All right, Mackin. Where were you?"

"In the store. Back in the office. Working on the books. A dozen people saw the light on. Now try somebody else. Maybe the Chief of Police did it."

"Be quiet, Billy," Paulson said. "MacReedy, I've got a lot of friends in this town. I don't care what you may think your legal rights are. You may have a hell of a lot less rights than you think. You've molested my daughter."

"She was willing to talk to me."

"I lost one girl. I'm not fixing to—"

"She was lost as far as you are concerned a long time before somebody killed her, Mr. Paulson. She was a lonely, mixed-up kid."

The butcher hands flexed. His voice was nearly a whisper, almost lost in the wind and the sound of the dry leaves. "She was evil. She was a foulness."

"Easy, Dick. Easy," Billy Mackin said, putting his hand on the older man's arm.

"And Nancy's spirit is broken," I said. "She hasn't got enough guts left to admit to herself that she hates you. The Landy boy was her last chance to get clear of you."

Paulson raised a fist as though to strike me. He did not raise it in the way a man usually raises a fist. He lifted it high, as though he held a mace, or a crusader's sword. He looked as though he wanted to strike me down into the earth. I stepped back. His expression changed. The white look changed to a gray pallor. He slumped and his mouth opened. He pressed a hand against his chest, under his heart. He took three tottering steps to the bench, Mackin supporting him, and sat down slowly, arms braced on his knees, chin on his chest.

Mackin looked at him, moved over to one side, motioned me toward him. I approached boldly.

"Lay off him. He hasn't been well. I don't care what games you want to play, but leave him out of them, and stay away from Nancy."

"That's an order?"

"I think you'd better get out of town."

"I don't intend to."

"You're not making any friends."

"It doesn't worry me."

He tilted his head and looked up at me. "That was quite an act, last night. An amateur act. I don't know what the hell you had in mind." The grin wrinkles were very evident around his eyes. There was a little nick in his chin where he had evidently cut himself shaving. He looked compact, handsome, plausible, likable. "Actually, MacReedy, and level with me now—did you have any crazy notion I'd killed that girl?"

I waited long seconds before I answered. I had the curious feeling of a man who, showing off for his girl, puts his hand inside the bars where a tiger is sleeping.

"I know you killed her, Mackin. And I know why."

There was no change of posture or expression. I thought I saw something shift behind his eyes. It was half seen. It made me remember a job we had in the southwest, in rattlesnake country. I was climbing a hill. The sun was so bright hot that it made the rocks blaze white and made the shadows deep and black. I saw the heavy shadow in a pocket of the rocks and I thought of snakes and as I had the thought I saw the hint of movement, a slight change in the shades of blackness. I fired into the pocket. The rattler came writhing, spasming out, slithering down the rocks, thick belly punctured. I put the third slug through his head.

This was the same. A slight shifting, a change in the colors of blackness.

Then he turned and spat and looked at me again and said, "Where do you take that needle? Right in the vein?"

"There's one thing you should know. So you can worry about it, Mackin. There'll be no execution on Monday."

"A score for your side? So it'll be a week from Monday. Do you think that's a kindness to the kid? It's a hell of a way to buy a ticket into Vicky's bed. You must be hard up, fella. This is friendly advice. I don't hold grudges. Dick does. You pack up and get out or there's going to be trouble, believe me."

I had nothing more to say to him. Dusk was beginning to thicken. I went back to the Inn. When I looked back, Billy was sitting next to Paulson on the bench, one hand on his shoulder.

After I had shaved and changed I hunted up Charlie. I had one question for him, and it grew into two. "How is Dick Paulson's health?"

"I don't really know. There's a rumor he has a bad heart. I don't know how bad it is, or if he's had an actual attack, but I do remember one lodge thing where we were advised not to initiate him. The lodge dreams up some pretty depressing stuff. Paulson has a lot of dignity. A humiliating initiation might have made him mad. And I hear he's supposed to avoid getting mad."

And I thought of my second question. "How well off is he?"

"Damn well off. He doesn't live up to it though, so few would think so. He doesn't have to do his own meat cutting. But he saves plenty by doing it. It isn't the store so much as the good real estate guesses he's made. Then he got into scrap as a sideline during the war. Sold his yard out at just the right moment. He's got five or six good farms I know of. And he's got a nice fat piece of the new shopping center. He's doing fine."

Once you start a train of thought, there are a lot more questions. "Billy Mackin started from nothing. I understand he didn't make it all himself."

"Angela had some money. About twenty thousand, I'd guess. Then I think Dick loaned him some when he put up the new building. I don't know how much or whether he's paid it back."

"I suppose you could say Dick has treated him like a son."

"That's pretty close. And you're close to sneering, Hugh. I don't get it. Billy is—"

"I know. He's a good joe. You told me."

"And he's having a bad time right now."

"Nobody has said anything at all about Mrs. Paulson. What's she like?"

Charlie sipped his beer and glanced at the clock. "I don't know. I don't think anybody knows. You'd have to meet her ten times before you could even come close to remembering her face. I think of her as being about ten shades of gray. Gray hair, dress, face, hands and conversation. I hear that long ago she was good looking and high spirited. You'd never know it. She does a lot of church work. She's— Hell, Hugh, she's a zombie. She acts one-tenth alive, and you think that if you yelled boo, she'd keel over."

"Suppose Paulson has put the lid on her?"

"I wouldn't figure him as the easiest man in the world to live with. Look at the clerks he's got. They either get to be mice or they don't stay."

"Jane Ann was the one he couldn't control."

"I think she was just as tough as he is."

"One thing more, and then I'll let you go. After the body was found, did Paulson get sick?"

"He didn't come back to the store for ten days. They kept it open and they couldn't get a butcher so they closed the meat department. He looked like hell when he came back. They say it nearly killed him."

"It could have?"

"If what I hear about his heart is true, it could have. But it didn't."

"Then suppose somebody told him about me and told him I was sitting in the park out there on a bench pumping Nancy, and pointed the two of us out and he came storming out and I got lippy with him, that could kill him too?"

"Maybe, if he got mad enough."

"Suppose that good joe, Billy Mackin, brought him out?"

Charlie looked injured. "Billy is in a better position to know how bad Dick's heart is. Did this really happen?"

"Just a little while ago. My act didn't go over with Mackin. He checked me out with Chief Score."

"Oh?"

"And just rattle this around in your head, Charlie. Maybe my act wasn't perfect, but it wasn't bad. So why shouldn't Mackin have taken me at face value? Why all the extra suspicion?"

He shook his head sorrowfully and clucked his tongue. "You are way, way out in left field."

"He's a good joe?"

"He hasn't got all the background in the world. He bummed around when he was a kid. But he's bright. Darn it all, Hugh, I know the guy. I've been drunk with him. I've played poker with him. I've served on committees with him. He'll work like a dog for anything that's for the good of the town. He knows how to tell a good story. Look, he's a nice guy."

"He likes the picture of himself as a pillar of the community. He works hard at it. He—We better skip it." Charlie stood up. I looked up at him. "I'm told to get out of town," I said.

"Again?"

"Think I should?"

"I know you won't, so I won't waste my breath."

Facts, guesses and suspicions were all jumbled

in my mind. I couldn't sort them out logically.
wanted to have things in better order before I saw
Vicky again. I had half promised I would be out to
see her in the evening. I had some solitary drinks
and ate a solitary meal. When I tried processes of
orderly thought and logical planning I realized the
cumulative strain of the past several days, the nervous tension, had impaired my powers of deduc-
tion. I wondered if Vicky could help. I would put
everything on the table and we would try to sort it
out together.

The thing that intrigued me most, more even
than my suspicions of the wider scope of Mackin's
motivations, was the strange seizure which had
turned Nancy into blinded rigidity. I wondered if
this was something that happened to her often.
Her father had seemed to treat it as something of
no importance. But then I realized that it was entirely possible that he had been unaware of it.
He might not have seen how she was from the
point where he had shouted her name. By the time
he took her arm and pulled her from the bench, she
had started to come out of it. It seemed reasonable
to suppose that this was not an ordinary thing. It
seemed like hysteria. And I knew that if Nancy
had been subject to such attacks, it would be
known and somebody would have told me—Vicky,
Ginny Garson, John Tennant, Don Higel—somebody.

I knew that the persistence of my questioning
had driven her into that curious state. And it was
related to Mackin.

I was lifting the coffee cup to my lips when I had
an idea that fit so perfectly there was practically

an audible click. I lowered the cup cautiously back to the saucer. My hand was shaking. I exhaled deeply. It all went with what John Tennant had said—about impressions lodging in the subconscious mind. Something Ginny Garson had said had made practically no impression on me at the time she had said it. Now it seemed important. It was when Ginny had been telling me of Jane Ann's spirited defense of her sister's prissiness. Jane Ann had told Ginny, without further explanation, that Nancy had a good reason for being that way. There could be a very good reason, and it could be associated with Mackin. It had to be.

I needed the services of a confirmed gossip, some nosy person who made everybody's business her business, and coupled curiosity with a good memory. As soon as I thought of the specifications, I remembered the mean and narrow face of Vicky's landlady, Mrs. Hemsold.

The wind had died and it did not seem as cold. The air was chill and tart and I decided to walk. There were no other pedestrians. Car tires made silk sounds on smooth asphalt. Mrs. Hemsold's lights were on. I hesitated in front of the house, wondering what possible approach I could use. She would not be willing to talk to me. I could think of no plan, and decided to try to take my cues from her.

She must have heard me come onto the porch because the light went on and the door was snatched open as I reached toward the bell. "Have you come about the apartme— It's you!"

"Yes. I wondered if you—"

"I have absolutely nothing to say to you, young man. You had better go back to that woman." She slammed the door hard and the light went out.

I pressed the bell button. I kept my thumb on it for a long time. The door opened just far enough for me to see that she had fastened a chain lock across it, just far enough for me to see a narrow slice of her bitter old face.

"If you aren't off my porch in ten seconds, young man, I'm going to call the police."

"I was told you could help me, Mrs. Hemsold."

"Help you? Help you what?"

I talked rapidly. "I know I could go to Mrs. Paulson, but I'm afraid this is the kind of thing that would upset her."

"What would upset Myra Paulson?"

"I was told you are a friend and a good neighbor of theirs, Mrs. Hemsold. I know you are a decent and honest woman, Mrs. Hemsold, and you would want to see justice done."

"I always try to do the right thing, young man. And I do not care to carry on a conversation with you. I saw you with her, carrying on with her. And you can stop beating around the bush. What is it you want?"

I took the gamble. In another moment she was going to slam the door again. "I want to ask you about Nancy Paulson's trouble."

"Trouble? I don't know what you're talking about."

I could hardly believe I'd drawn a blank. "I'm sorry, Mrs. Hemsold. I guess you never heard about it."

"Oh! I know what you mean. *That* trouble. Land

that was, let me see, seven years ago."

"Do we have to talk through the door? I assure you I'm an honest and reliable person."

"Why should I let you in my house? And anyway, what does that trouble have to do with you?"

"I'm not very good at making speeches, Mrs. Hemsold. I know that everybody is convinced Alister Landy is guilty. But we all owe a debt to society to try to trace down and eliminate every last shred of doubt. That's the Christian thing to do."

"I don't— Oh, now I see, but that is ridiculous! Do you mean to say that you think the same person could have been responsible? Heavens above, young man, you must be out of your mind."

"But don't you see that I can't know how ridiculous it is until I get the story from somebody who really knows?"

I saw the war between moral indignation, and the desire of a lonely old woman to gossip. It was more skirmish than war. The door closed. The chain rattled and then it swung wide. "You might as well come in. My duty, as I see it, is to keep you from spreading malicious rumors about that sweet child. Now that you're in, you might as well come all the way in and sit down."

The old fashioned living-room was spotless. The wood gleamed with oil, wax and many polishings. There was a great abundance of embroidery and needlepoint. She sat in the rocker facing me.

"I want you to understand," I said, "this is painful to me. I thought a long time before imposing on you. I assure you that I—"

"Nancy is a lovely child and I wouldn't have her

hurt for the world. I'll tell you about it so that it won't have to go any farther. You'll see how ridiculous your ideas are. I'll never understand how two children of the same parents raised the same way can be so different. Jane Ann was trash. No good at all. Oh, they want to cover that all up now and forget it, but I could tell you some things if I had a mind to. But I'm not one to gossip about my neighbors. I've prayed for Jane Ann's soul. Different as night and day, those two girls. Nancy sings in the church, you know. Mr. Hemsold, before he passed away, was a deacon. He was in the lumber business. I hope, wherever he is, he doesn't look down often and see me having to rent part of the lovely house he built for me, just to make ends meet. Nancy has such a clear, lovely voice. It's like an angel singing. You never heard the like. She's always been a more delicate child than Jane Ann was. Land, you could tell that just by looking at the two of them. It doesn't seem fair that it should have been Nancy to have that trouble; but when you think about it I guess it's better she had that trouble than have happen to her what happened to Jane Ann; but I'm willing to say right here and now that Jane Ann was begging for what happened to her. She should have known some men are just beasts that happen to walk on their hind legs. This trouble was all hushed up, you know, and very few people ever heard about it, and some of them are dead, God rest their souls. It was a terrible, terrible thing and many is the afternoon Myra Paulson was over here sitting right there on the couch where you're sitting, crying her eyes out about it because the poor child was only eleven. It's

a terrible thing to happen to a poor little child and
it is God's blessing she didn't lose her mind over
it—Nancy, I mean. It was on a Labor Day week
end. Dick Paulson and Billy Mackin had been
working hard that summer building a camp together up at Morgan's Lake. They had some of the
local people up there working on it too, but Dick
and Billy got away every chance they had and
pitched in. Labor Day is a time, you know, when a
lot of the city riffraff get into their old cars and go
up to the lakes. When she was tiny Nancy was a
great one for wandering off by herself and finding
things like flowers and berries and bird feathers
and bringing them back for a kind of collection she
had. Seven years ago that west shore of the lake
wasn't built up near as much as it is now. I hear it's
getting too built up, with camps practically one on
top of the other, but that's neither here nor there.
Nancy wandered off that day and nobody thought
too much about it on account of she was always a
quiet child and she could amuse herself and she
spent a lot of time alone. Well, she didn't come
back for lunch and then Dick and Myra were annoyed and then they got worried. I can tell you that
by late afternoon there were an awful lot of folks
out tramping through the woods, looking for her
and calling out her name. They found her two
miles from the camp, back toward the hills, walking around just like she was walking in her sleep.
Her clothes were all tore and her throat was
bruised something terrible. She didn't make out
she could recognize her own people, and she
couldn't talk or even cry. They knew it was some
man did it, and the poor child was just scared wit-

less. The doctors said she'd been choked unconscious and left for dead, and they found it hadn't happened to her. You know. Like maybe the man heard a noise and got scared off or something. But as far as the effect on her is concerned, the worst might just as well have happened. She'd been such a merry little thing, and it was like she went under a cloud. She lost a whole semester of school, but she made that up. But you know, she wasn't the same child any more. She turned out scary. The Paulsons wanted it all hushed up, so they put her in a sort of a rest home way over the other side of Warrentown and told everybody she was off visiting Myra's sister but some of us were let in on the true story. The police worked quiet, and they investigated all kinds of drunks and vagrants they picked up in the lake country, but they couldn't find the man who did it. She's a lovely, lovely girl now; but it did make a cloud for her to live under. It is purely God's blessing that the terror drove all the memory of it right out of her mind. But even so, it left its mark. So you can see, young man, that was a long time ago and a long ways from here that it happened. Anybody who tries to say it was the same man attacked both the Paulson girls is way out of their head, and you can take that for gospel. I don't agree with what you're trying to do, and I didn't want you here in my house, but I felt it was my bounden duty to tell you the truth so you wouldn't go hollering off on the wrong track."

"I certainly appreciate your courtesy, Mrs. Hemsold."

"Nancy is a lovely child and we all wish her all the best in life. I, for one, feel that what happened so Jane Ann was for the best. Had she lived, she would have given Dick and Myra nothing but heartbreak for the rest of their lives. Now they've got one lovely daughter left, and they can be proud of her, believe me. I'm not one to make any guesses without good reason, but I can see what's ahead for that girl."

"What do you mean?"

She made a little smacking sound with her lips and looked at me with great satisfaction. "Fate moves in mysterious ways, young man, and when you get older you'll begin to see how there's a pattern in everything. I don't know if you've seen Angela Mackin over to the store or if you'd know who she was if you saw her. But if you saw her, you wouldn't forget her in a hurry. That woman is walking death, believe me. She hasn't got long to go, and there's some say she's doesn't know it, but I'd wager she's got a pretty good idea. She and Billy never had any children, and I guess now Billy is glad they didn't, even though he wanted them so bad. There's some who hold to the old fashioned ways, but I say the world is changing day by day and it's up to us to change right along with it. You mark my words, young man, there's going to be a wedding and I say Billy shouldn't wait over six months after Angela is in her grave. Nancy'll be nineteen soon and if I ever saw two people that need each other and are right for each other, those are the two. Nancy needs love and understanding and tenderness, and Billy is going to need a young and loving and pretty wife so's he can forget watching Angela go down hill all these long months. It'll be a good thing all around. Nancy can stay right in the neighborhood, practically next door, and that'll be so much easier on her people than if she were to marry and go away and leave them all alone. Maybe some would call it sinful for me to talk this way with Angela not even in her coffin yet, but a body has to face up to facts and do the best they can. Dick Paulson's heart is in terrible bad shape and it would be a tragedy if Nancy were to go away now. You know, Billy Mackin even comes over and does Dick's yard work for him, and he hasn't got time left to take decent care of his own yard. I can see the handwriting on the wall and it's going to work out for the best. Mr. Hemsold was eleven years older than me, and I must say we had a very happy life together until he died in nineteen thirty-eight on Friday the thirteenth at quarter to eight in the morning. I called him for breakfast and he always came down those front stairs there to get the paper and take it out to the kitchen. I heard the stairs squeaking and then there was all the thumping and I ran in and he was right there near that mat you can see from where you're sitting. Dr. Farbon said it was a stroke and he never felt a thing, and you could well believe it from the peaceful look on his face. He left everything in perfect order, and I guess he died thinking I'd be well fixed for the rest of my life but he didn't know how prices were going to go up out of sight. I think a husband should be older, and Billy will be a good steady husband for Nancy, better than some dreamy boy who thinks the world owes him a living. And, you know, I think Nancy will be happy to marry him. Don't you get the idea they've been making up to each other or anything. Billy is too fine a young man to try and fiddle-de-dee with Angela dying on his hands. Nancy acts scairt of all men, but on account of Billy being such a good friend and knowing him so long, she'll be easier with him than with anybody."

"Has anybody mentioned it, or are you just guessing?"

She looked as if I had insulted her. "Guessing! When you get older you begin to see the pattern in things. Nobody has come right out and said it would happen, but I've got ears and eyes. Many a day Myra stops over and we have tea. Mr. Hemsold was born in Southampton, England, and he had tea every living day of his life and he taught me to like it too. From what she's said, and understand she didn't say anything *right out,* Dick has been thinking on Billy being a good match for Nancy later on. Now let me tell you I've known Dick Paulson since the time he used to deliver groceries right here to this same house, back when he was a raggedy, solemn little boy right down off the farm over near Bluebird after his folks died of the typhoid. That was back when it was Cal White's market, and I bet Cal had no idea of Dickie Paulson taking over the place and a lot of other things besides. And I can tell you one thing about Dick. Anything he sets his mind to, it comes true sooner or later, you mark my words."

She stood up abruptly. "I've done my Christian duty and might as well go now, young man, or I'll start saying things you'll have no liking to hear. I hear the Landy woman has gone clean away from town but if you see her you can tell her for me and the other decent folks around here that she won't be welcome if she tries to come back."

When I turned and tried to thank her she slammed the door. The porch light went off before I was down the steps. I walked slowly back to the Inn. Many things had fallen into place. I felt that I could understand Jane Ann a little more. She would have been nine when that happened to her sister. And all of a sudden her sister seemed to be getting all of the love and attention in the household. It would not be impossible for Jane Ann to have gotten some distorted idea of what had happened. And that could account for her wayward-ness, her experimentations. They had been not only a protest but a curious way to try to regain the love and attention that was all being given to her sister.

I did not go into the Inn. I went aound to get into my car. There was no outside light at the small parking area. Some light came through the back windows of the Inn. At first he was a shadow that detached itself from a dark car parked near mine.

And then he was a breath in my face, tainted with whisky and vomit.

"Still meddling around, you son of a bitch," he said thickly.

"You're drunk, Quillan."

"Not too drunk, you bastard. You and Perry. Both bastards. He smells trouble. So he cuts him-self loose. He fires me. Your fault, you big-mouth bastard. I think I'm going to kill you."

And if he had hit me with that first punch, hit me where he wanted to hit me, he might have killed me right then. I got my left arm up barely in time. His fist numbed my arm. I turned from the expected knee, and it caught me on the thigh, knocking me back against my car.

He rushed me, and I tried to slip free. He caught me on the forehead with a wild swing. Liquor had dulled his reflexes. For a moment he was silhouetted against the light. I hit him as hard and as fast and as cleanly as I could, three blows to the face, right, left, right. I put meat into the last one. I've hit people that hard before. They've gone down. He rushed me again and I backed up fast, backed out from between the cars to where I had more room.

He came heavily out into the open. I circled him slowly. There was the sound of our shoes on the gravel, our breathing, a distant sound of music. I hit him twice more, but not as hard, because I was trying to stay away from him. He did not try to hit back. At the second blow, his fingers slipped off my wrist before he could get a good grip. In the faint light the blood on his mouth looked black. I knew he wanted to get hold of me. And I knew I wouldn't stand much chance if he did. Discretion said turn and run like hell. But it isn't pretty to run from a man.

"Kill you," he said indistinctly.

He dived for my legs. I skipped sideways and he rolled over and over. When he came up to his feet, I had slipped around behind him. I clasped my fists together and struck him on the nape of the neck as hard as I could. I expected him to go down again, but he whirled with agility I hadn't expected, and I was too off balance to skitter back. He got my arm.

I hit him twice around the eyes with my left fist,
but he pulled me close, locked his arms around me,
fists on the small of my back, his shoulder pressing
against my throat.

We were motionless for a moment, and then he
increased the pressure. I heard the audible creak
of my ribs. All the air was pushed out of my lungs.
He bent me, and the sky grew darker, and I knew
he was crazy enough to keep it up until my back
snapped. I tried to get hold of his hair but it was too
short. I got one hand up and around and down to
his face. He tried to snuggle his face into my neck,
but I got the tips of my first and second fingers into
his nostrils and pulled up and back. The pressure
didn't cease. I pulled until I felt the sickening rip of
tissue. He grunted with pain and the pressure
went and I could breathe. As I sucked air in, he hit
me. There was no sense of falling. I did not feel
myself hit the ground, but I recovered almost at
once. He was on me, knee like a keg smashing my
stomach with his entire weight. There was enough
light there so that when he stabbed at my eye with
a thumbnail, I turned and took a gash on the side
of my face. I knew he meant to blind me. I struck at
his face. He locked his hands on my throat. I had
an instant of time in which to tighten all the muscles of my throat. Had I not done so, the first violent pressure would have mashed my throat, killed
me in that instant. I flailed my arms, writhed,
tried to get enough leverage to buck and throw
him off. But his knee pinned me. My hand struck
something, turned, curled around it. I pulled it
free of the ground. The edge of the parking lot was

marked by bricks set cornerwise into the ground and whitewashed.

The sky had darkened again and I could not see him. I struck and felt the brick hit. I struck five times, and though I was trying to use all my strength, I felt as though my arm were a tube of cotton, the brick a sponge.

The big hands turned slack without warning. He collapsed onto me. I felt his blood on my face. I had to wait until I could move. I pushed him off. He rolled onto his back. I sat up and buried my face against my knees. Each deep breath made a whistling sound. The left side of my face felt numb. When I tried to swallow, my throat felt full of those metal jacks little girls play games with. When I got up I wavered and went down to one knee and got up again. I found my lighter. I squatted beside him and lit it. His face was spoiled. Blood ran from his ear. I did not like the look of that. It was not a good thing. I tried to find his pulse. His wrist was too meaty. I put my ear on his chest. It sounded much too thin and fast and sharp. His heart sounded as if it were trying to peck its way out of his chest.

By luck I managed to get to my room without being seen. I washed the blood off. I changed my suit and shirt. I put tape on the ragged gouge near my eye. There was no other mark. It seemed miraculous. I looked at a stranger in the mirror. I felt as if I were in seven pieces, and the man in the mirror looked calm. I got the revolver, took it out of the holster, put it and a box of shells in my side pocket. I went down to the phone booth in the back of the entrance hall. I found the number for Dr. Higel. I paused, changed my mind, called John Tennant first.

"I've got no time to chat," I said. "Quillan jumped me behind the Inn. Nobody saw it. I don't know whether I killed him. I may have. Let Arma know."

"Have you called a doctor?"

"I called you first."

"Call a doctor. Wait by Quillan until he comes. Turn yourself in. I'll be there in fifty minutes."

"I'll call the doctor. Then I'm leaving. I've got things to do."

"Hugh, don't be a damn—"

I didn't hear the rest because I had hung up. I phoned Dr. Don Higel at his home. His voice was brisk and alert when he answered. "This is Mac-Reedy," I said.

"What now?"

"Quillan is in back of the Inn, in the parking lot. He jumped me. He may be dying. He may be dead by now."

"Wait there," he said.

I hung up on him. I hurried out and got into the car. When I swung around my headlights stopped on Quillan. He hadn't moved. I had an impulse to run the car over him. It was so strong it frightened me. I wanted to feel the car jounce over him. I missed him. I was ten miles from town in ten minutes.

Chapter 11

WHEN VICKY OPENED THE DOOR I had every intention of being calm, factual, controlled. She opened the door and I opened my mouth but no words came. When I stepped inside, my knees sagged, but I caught myself. I felt faint. I leaned too heavily on her. She helped me to the bed. I sat down and looked up at her and tried to smile. Her face was vivid with concern, anxiety.

"What's happened, Hugh? What has happened? Tell me, darling."

It was a few moments before I could speak. I was ashamed of my own weakness. I've been in bad spots before. It is always the same. The trembles come later. And they don't last long. I've been in a tunnel when some of the roof came down and the shoring began to creak and shift. I've been on a mountain road when the master cylinder quit and there were no more brakes. But Quillan had been something else—bare-handed murder, undeviating intent. Maybe when he sobered up after killing me, he would have been very sorry about the whole thing, very remorseful. And if that brick had been six inches further away, I would have already begun my share of eternity.

I told her. She insisted on bathing and rebandaging the thumbnail gouge near my eye. She did not work gingerly or tentatively. She did it with the quickness of a good nurse. Then she got a cold damp towel and I held it against the numbed side of my face. She insisted that I stretch out. She unlaced my shoes and pulled them off. She wanted to know if I had told anyone where she was, so they could come after me. I had told no one.

After she had fixed the light so it didn't shine in my eyes, and after she had hung the jacket of my suit on a hanger in the closet, she sat on the bed, one knee akimbo, ankle resting on her other knee, and said, "Now tell me all the rest, Hugh."

I didn't talk for a moment. I just looked at her. There was enough light behind her to halo her dark hair. She wore some kind of lounging slacks, tightfitting, flared at the low slung ankles. They were a burnt orange hue. She wore a white shiny shirt with a Chinese collar, full sleeves, tight cuffs. She wore flat sandals with narrow white straps.

"What's the matter?" she asked, looking uncomfortable.

"You're very good to look at, Vicky."

"I—I bought these today. There's a shop down the way. This sort of thing is not my usual dish of tea. I feel a little theatrical. I thought it would be good for morale."

"Mine?"

"Please, Hugh. What did happen?"

I went through all the rest of the things that had happened. I had planned to keep it factual, but I could not help getting off into personal conjecture, subjective evaluation of the facts. It seemed to take quite a long time to finish.

"Then this is what you believe," she said. "You believe Mackin had a double motive. He is legally murdering his own wife. He had to get rid of Jane Ann. Maybe, in addition to the blackmail, she would never have permitted her sister to marry him. You think he has his sights on Nancy. That was why he went to such extremes to make it look as if Al had done it. And you believe that, seven years ago, it was Mackin who attacked Nancy when she was a child."

It seemed as good a time as any, so I told her about the card that had been tossed into Frank Leader's car, how I had found out about it, and what Tennant planned to do with the information. Her reaction startled me. Ever since I had seen her at Mrs. Hemsold's house, there had been a darkness in her. I knew part of it was resentment at me and the way I had treated her long ago. But most of it was despair at what was happening to her brother.

Her face changed suddenly. She was a lost and hungry child who had somehow found her way home, and found everybody waiting with ice cream and cake. It was as though a light went on behind her blue eyes, and it made her whole face luminous. I knew then that she had, for the first time, completely accepted my unproven suspicions of Billy Mackin. For the first time in dreary months she knew the quick taste of hope.

She was quite still for a moment, eyes glowing, lips apart. Then her face crumpled just a little and she flung herself against me with strange awkwardness for one who always moved so lithely. As I held her and as she wept I acquired a deeper understanding of the strain she had been under. Her body quivered and tears like hot wax fell against the side of my throat.

My only intent had been to hold her and comfort her and try to share what strength I had. But we were vulnerable, both of us. Unlike the last time together, this was not the result of any sly and careful campaign. If there was blame, indeed if there was any cause for blame, it had to be shared equally. There was no sudden change. Mood shifted and meshed into another mood. Small fires glowed and then flamed up. There had been no need for words. There were no restraints, no hesitations. We shared each other without words, meeting with such a great need, such a wonderful sensitization to each other that it could have been the second thousandth time we had been with each other rather than the second. The great need made for quickness, and then there was a half slumberous time like a glow of embers, and then the rise of need again, and it lasted long. Very long. That was the best of it, the long way it went and the long time it lasted.

When she left me, she left quickly, and I heard the click of the latch of the bathroom door. I turned on the bed lamp, and I dressed. I knew that never again would there be time in my life for the brassy ones, the bold ones, the coarse ones. I had taken this strange dark girl of shyness and passion and her I would keep.

The orange slacks lay crumpled beside the bed. I

found a hanger for them, and I picked up the rest of her clothing.

When she came out of the bathroom she was wearing a pale gray robe. It made her eyes look very blue in the moment she glanced at me and looked away, her face turning pink. Her feet were bare. She looked very small. She had scrubbed her face, combed her hair, replaced her lipstick. She came up to me, head bent, hooked her fingertips in my belt and leaned her forehead against my chest. I looked down at the clean white part in her black hair.

"Sorry?" she whispered.

"What a ridiculous question. I should ask it."

"I'm not sorry. I thought of it happening again and thought I would be ashamed of letting it happen again. Ashamed of being weak and wanting you. I'm not ashamed." She leaned up suddenly and brushed her lips across mine and turned away to say, far too casually, over her shoulder. "But I'm all grown up now. I've gotten over a lot of stupid ideas, darling. This time there are no obligations."

"Come now!" I said softly. "Stick to the script. Demand marriage. You're a betrayed maiden. Don't turn into a sophisticate on me."

She whirled and leaned against the dressing table. "Now don't tease. I was very young—that first time."

"I think I was the younger one."

"No obligations. I insist."

"All right, then. None. No obligations at all for this time. But I owe you for the first time. Remember the way I didn't say it when you were waiting to hear it? I love you. See? It's easy to say. Marry me. That's easy too."

She shook her head. "No answers yet, Hugh. Not until things are—settled."

"They will be."

"I could almost believe you. What if Quillan is dead? Then both of you will be—in that place."

"I won't be. His threat is on record. Arma took it down."

"But what do we do?" she asked, moving toward me.

"We start thinking. And the first step is you go right back where you were and you stay over there and I'll try not to look at you too long or too often."

She made a face and went back to the dressing table and sat on the bench in front of it. We thought out loud. I paced. I went through four cigarettes. I tried to sum up our progress. "Okay. Maybe Nancy could discredit him if she could remember. But it was such a bad shock to her it drove the whole incident underground. She has no conscious memory of it. The only symptom she showed was that queer kind of trance she went into."

Vicky bit her lip. "Hugh—is it like—this sounds weird—combat fatigue? I mean I read about some of the men in the war not remembering. Didn't they give them drugs and then they could talk?"

I thought that over. "Fine. Just slip her the needle. How do we go about that? Ask Paulson? 'Dick, we want to give Nancy a little jolt of this here mystery drug. You hold her.'"

"But, darling, you said you liked Don Higel so

well and he seemed to like you. Wouldn't he co-operate?"

"That's a hell of a thing to ask him, Vicky."

"But we could do one thing, couldn't we? We could at least tell him about all this and tell him how Nancy acted and see if he thinks our guess is right."

I sighed. "It's a starting place. Suppose you go to bed. I'll go make myself unpopular with Higel."

"I'm coming with you."

"You're staying here, Vicky."

"This time I'm going to be with you."

"No!"

Don Higel had built his office onto the front of a small frame house not far from the business area of the village. After I had checked his garage and found the station wagon gone, and had seen no lights in office or home, I went back to the car and moved it down the street into a dark place where the street lights were dim.

"What do we do now?" Vicky asked.

"Wait for him. I can't think of anything else to do. Cigarette?"

"Please."

We waited for twenty-five minutes. Don Higel turned into his driveway at twenty minutes after two. He drove into the garage. When he came wearily out to pull down the overhead door, I stepped out of the shadows, startling him.

"Oh—it's you."

"How is Quillan?"

"He's in Warrentown General with a fractured skull, multiple abrasions and lacerations."

"Serious?"

"He'll live, Hugh. Your lawyer was here. He left in disgust. You aren't his favorite client. And the police want a nice chat with you."

"He was trying to kill me, Don."

"I suppose so. Want some coffee?"

"I'll be leaving a lady out in the cold. I do want to talk to you."

He looked toward my car. "Who is it?"

"Vicky Landy."

He sighed. "Go get her. This looks like a longer night than I thought it was going to be."

Don and I sat at the kitchen table. Vicky made coffee and toast. When I began my story he looked bored. He became very alert when I started to talk about Nancy. It was as though he had snapped to attention. Several times he seemed on the verge of interrupting me. I finished up by saying, "That's the story. We know Alister is innocent. But we need the information Nancy has. And I think it's locked away where we can't touch it. I know this is asking a lot, but we wondered if there's any way you could help us, Don."

Vicky was sitting across from me. Don ordered her to put her fingers in her ears. Then he cursed fluently, emphatically, for at least thirty seconds. We stared at him.

"What's the matter?" I asked when he had slowed down.

"Matter? The matter is that some stupid people seem to think it's necessary to conceal facts from the family doctor." He shoved his chair back and got up. "Am I supposed to carry a crystal ball? You know where I've come from? Right from the Paulson house. Two patients. Nancy and her father."

We both stared at him. He sat down. The anger went out of him. "I could take care of Paulson. I've treated him before. I keep him under constant sedation. But when he gets too excited, he gets another attack. Auricular fibrillation. Then he'll run a pulse over two hundred until I can knock it down."

"Will it kill him?" I asked.

"Eventually. There's some damage, of course. It puts a hell of a load on the heart. Maybe some time I won't be able to stop it and it will quit from pure muscular exhaustion. The extreme remedy is to go in there and grasp the heart and stop it for a moment and hope that when the beat continues it will be somewhere near normal. I treated him this afternoon. I stopped in at midnight after another house call, just to check. He was sleeping. The rate was way down when I checked it. I'd given him enough to keep him out for twenty-four hours. That'll give it a chance to rest. I started to leave. Mrs. Paulson, acting scared to death, asked me to look at Nancy. She said her husband wouldn't approve of her asking me to take a look at her, but she said she was worried. And I damn well didn't blame her.

"The girl was in bed and her room lights were out. Mrs. Paulson turned on the lights. She was on her back, eyes open, staring at the ceiling. Pulse, respiration and temperature were all subnormal. She would follow simple orders. Semi-catatonic. Very little response. Lift her hand over her head and release it and she would hold it there, and then slowly let it come down. Her pupils responded very slowly to light. I suspected dementia praecox. It hits often at that age. Withdrawal. Out of my field. She seemed to be highly suggestible. I closed her eyes and ordered her to sleep. She went into a deep sleep almost immediately. Then I went downstairs with Mrs. Paulson and questioned her. No, Nancy hadn't been acting strange lately. There had been some kind of trouble in the afternoon. Some man annoying her. Mr. Paulson hadn't given her the details. Nancy had acted queer and far away ever since she had come home. She hadn't eaten. I knew, of course, that she'd had some severe emotional shocks—her boy friend killing her sister. I guessed this was a delayed reaction. I told Mrs. Paulson I'd arrange for a Warrentown man to come over and examine her tomorrow. Rikert. He's good. So now, damn it, I find out why."

"Can you do anything?"

"The best word I can think of for her condition is hysteria. She has an insoluble problem, Hugh. She's been far too subservient to her father's will. She has been the 'good' child, and Jane Ann was the 'bad' child. You prodded subconscious memories. Enough of that memory came to the surface to put her into this condition. I think she's been fed enough nonsense about her father's heart to feel that if she remembers the whole incident, it will kill her father. Yet there is love and sympathy for Alister. She has tried to bury that. Maybe she senses a relationship between the buried incident and the death of her sister. Here is what will happen to her. She may drift from hysteria into a complete withdrawal, into clinical mental illness. Or perhaps she can be forced to face the hidden incident and relive it."

"Can you force her to do that?"

"I don't know. I don't know."

"Can you try?"

"I can try. She's suggestible enough so I could attempt hypnosis first, try an age regression technique on her if she responds. Then scopolamine if that doesn't work. The trouble is, I may be meddling. I could do her more harm than good. And another thing, people. Even though hypnosis is an accredited medical technique and used one hell of a lot more often than you'd think, if word gets around that young Doctor Higel is using it, my practice here will go thud. Even so, I have the feeling the sooner we do it the better. Look, you pour yourselves some more coffee. I'm going to see what Rikert thinks."

After he left the kitchen Vicky reached over and squeezed my hand hard.

"Keep your fingers crossed," I said.

The minutes seemed very long. At last Don Higel came back. His face seemed to sag with weariness behind the brave mustache. I could tell nothing from his expression. He sat and sipped his cooling coffee.

"Rikert wasn't too happy about three a.m. consultations," he said. "The case interests him. That's pure luck. He wants to do it himself. Tomorrow morning. I mean this morning. At eight o'clock. We'll take her over there. He'll be at the Hillbrook Sanitarium. I told him that there were legal matters involved, and asked him if he would mind an audience. He said he wouldn't mind at all.

I imagine you both want to be there. Her mother will have to be there. Who else do you want?"

"John Tennant," Vicky said.

"And a man named Arma," I added. "With the State Police."

"I'll drive the girl and her mother over. You better come separately."

We had two and a half hours' sleep at the motel, and I drove between the stone pillars and up the curving drive of the Hillbrook Sanitarium at ten after eight. When we asked for Doctor Rikert, the receptionist directed us down a long corridor to a waiting-room at the end of the corridor. There was a morning clatter of breakfast trays, a hospital odor of disinfectant and medication, the starched whisper of nurses, soft code bells sounding from the corridor speakers.

John Tennant and Larry Arma were in the waiting-room. They stood up when we came in. We were all known to each other. We talked in the hushed tones you use in any hospital.

"What's going on now?" I asked John.

"The girl is in there with her mother and the two doctors and a nurse. I don't know what they're doing to her. The older one—Rikert—said they'd tell us when we could come in. What's this all about, Hugh?"

"Is it a secret?" Arma asked.

"I don't want to try to explain. I want you to just listen. It might not work. It may mean a waste of time."

"You wasted a hell of a lot of my time last night, Hugh," John said heavily.

"I apologized on the phone."

"You don't have anything to worry about on the Quillan thing," Arma said.

Don Higel came out and closed the door behind him. He could not have had any more sleep than we had, but he looked as refreshed and alert as Vicky did. "He's bringing her along nicely," he said. "It shouldn't be much longer now. Her mother made quite a fuss, but she's quieted down now. It's a fascinating thing to watch. He's an expert. I've been learning a lot."

"Will I be able to take notes, Doctor?" Larry Arma asked.

"Of course."

The nurse opened the door and nodded. We filed in. Mrs. Paulson was seated at the left. She gasped audibly when she recognized Vicky. She started to say something in a high, thin, whining voice but the nurse hurried to her and whispered to her and she retreated into a sulky silence. Nancy sat in an arm chair that looked comfortable. The blinds were closed against the morning sunlight and her back was to the windows. Her arms rested on the arms of the chair. Her head was back, eyes open but unfocused, lips parted, breathing deep and slow, the lower part of her face curiously slack.

Doctor Rikert was a stocky, powerful man with black hair carefully and intricately combed to disguise incipient baldness. His jowls were so heavy as to give his face a square look. His brows were heavy and black, his expression one of alert and vital intelligence. He nodded briskly at us and spoke in a resonant voice far too loud for the hush of the room. He seemed to appreciate an audience.

"Please take those chairs there. This a very good subject, very receptive. We find our best subjects among adolescent females of sensitivity and a good order of intelligence. She cannot hear me now. She cannot hear any sound at all. When I speak her name she will hear that and from then on she will hear only my voice, so you may speak freely among yourselves if you care to do so.

"There were certain difficulties. I had to bring her out of a semi-comatose state to full awareness before I could place her properly in a hypnotic trance. This is a deep trance. Somnambulistic. I've given her the standard tests. She has been responding nicely to age regression techniques. Her mother has verified the accuracy of her memory. I understand from Doctor Higel that her hysteria results from an incident that happened on a Labor Day week end when she was eleven years old. The memory block may be too great. I believe we are about ready to determine that."

He moved close to her. "Nancy! You can hear me now and you will answer my questions. Your sleep is very deep, but you can hear me and you can answer me. How old are you, Nancy?"

The slack lips moved, became more firm. "Four—teen." Her voice was so slow we had to strain to hear. Her tone was thin and childish.

"Now you are going to become younger, Nancy. You are going to become smaller and younger, and you are going to answer my questions. Now you are thirteen. When I speak to you again, you will be twelve years old. Now you are twelve years old, Nancy. In a moment, when I speak to you again, you will be eleven years old. Now I speak to you again and you are eleven years old, Nancy. Eleven years old and you can talk to me and you can answer my questions. You will answer my questions. What is your favorite dress? What color is it? What is the color of your favorite dress?"

". . .Blue."

"Do you have a favorite dolly? What is the name of your favorite dolly, Nancy? What is her name?"

". . .Alice."

"Stop!" Mrs. Paulson cried. "Oh, please stop!" The nurse went to her again, sat beside her, held her hand. Dr. Rikert gave her one look of annoyance and continued.

"Now it is summer, Nancy, and you are eleven years old. Soon you will be going back to school. It is summer and you are at Morgan's Lake and pretty soon you will have to go back to school. Who is at the lake with you, Nancy?"

"Mommy and Jane Ann. . .and Aunt Angela."

"Where is your father?"

"He works in the store. Uncle Billy works in the store too. In a different store."

Her answers were less hesitant; but her voice was still light, childish, barely audible.

"Now it is Labor Day and your father and your Uncle Billy are working on the camp. What are they doing?"

". . .Hammering. On the roof."

"But you like to take walks in the woods? Do you like to take walks in the woods?"

". . .Yes." For the first time there was a troubled

expression on the placid face.

"Now you are walking by yourself in the woods. Is it a nice day?"

"Warm day."

"You are walking in the woods and you are happy. Are you happy?"

"Yes."

"Now, Nancy, I am going to ask you to tell me a story. I am going to ask you to tell me about a bad thing that happened while you were walking in the woods. It will be hard for you to tell me, but you are going to tell me because I want you to tell me. You will tell me about the bad thing that happened."

There was a long silence. Her lips moved. She did not speak.

"Now you are ready to tell me, Nancy. You will tell me now. When I count to three, you will be ready to tell me about the bad thing."

Again the silence. When he seemed about to speak to her again she said in a pale thin voice, "I am walking. I have a feather. I have a blue feather from a blue bird."

Her hand moved. Rikert said quickly, "You are deep asleep. You will stay asleep until I awaken you. Tell me about the bad thing."

When she spoke again I felt the stir of hair at the back of my neck, a prickling on the backs of my hands. "Daddy?" she said, in the loudest tone she had used. "Is that . . . Hello, Uncle Billy." She waited for his response. "It's a feather, see? A blue feather. . . . No, I'm going to give it to Mommy. . . . Give it back! You let me have it! . . . You *spoiled* it! See? You're bad. . . . What are you doing? Don't do

that! I don't like that! You stop it! Stop it or I'll tell!
. . . I don't want you to give me another doll. I'm
going to tell what you did. . . . Stop it! You're hurting my arm! You're hurting me! No. No! Don't!
Don't!" She had begun to writhe and twist in the
chair, her head rolling back and forth. And then,
in a shocking, gasping, screaming voice she
shouted, "*Mommeeee! Mom . . .*"

The sound stopped with a brutal abruptness.
She slumped sideways in the chair, hands moving
spasmodically, and held in a most curious way, as
though she clasped the wrists of hands that held
her throat. Her face darkened and I realized she
had stopped breathing.

Rikert slapped her cheek with his fingertips.
"Nancy! The story is over. Nancy! Now you are
deep asleep and the story is over and you are quiet
and you are not afraid."

Her hands dropped slowly back to the arms of
the chair. She breathed deeply. Her face relaxed. I
realized I was standing and I had taken two steps
toward the girl. I went back to my chair. Mrs.
Paulson's hands covered her face. Vicky was chalk
pale. Arma looked as though he had tasted something bitter. John Tennant sat with his eyes shut,
his lips moving, as though he prayed.

"Now you will sleep for two minutes. You will be
sound asleep, a deep, restful, refreshing sleep.
When I count to three you will go to sleep and be
deep asleep for two minutes and you will not be
able to hear anything, not even my voice, until I
speak your name again. One. Two. Now go into the
deep warm sleep. Three."

He turned his back on her. "That was quite rugged," he said. "That was quite a response. Do you people have what you need?"

"God, yes," Tennant said.

I could hear the quiet sound of Mrs. Paulson as she wept. I took Vicky's hand. It was like ice.

"Will she remember any of this?" Tennant asked.

"I could arrange it either way," Rikert said. "I think it will be best if she does remember. It's been buried long enough. We may get a violent reaction when she awakens, and I may have to use sedation. I'll instruct her to remember everything when I wake her up. I'll want to keep her here a few days. There's no reason for you people to watch the rest of this. Don, I want you to stay. And Mrs. Paulson, of course."

We walked through the clean sunlight to where I had parked the car. Vicky shuddered visibly and said, "Ugly. Ugly."

"There's nothing uglier. It must have given Mackin a horrible turn when he found out he hadn't killed her. And he must have sweated for a long, long time before he was certain her memory wouldn't return."

"He was lucky."

"And now I think he's fresh out of luck."

Tennant joined us at the car. "I think I know where we go from here," he said. "I have a half-baked plan of procedure. It needs a lot of work. We'll need the girl, I think, for the *coup de théâtre*. Miss Landy, the first step is to get a stay of execution for your brother. And that, I am afraid, may be the easiest part of this thing. The next step is a conference, Hugh. A conclave. Miss Landy, if the

way you look at this tangle-footed specimen is any
indication, he has my premature congratulations.
See you in my office at two this afternoon,
Hugh."

He walked away. I kissed the blushing Miss
Landy.

Chapter 12

AT ELEVEN-THIRTY ON A CLOUDY WEDNESDAY MORN-
ING, two days after Alister Landy had been origi-
nally slated to die, a group was assembled in a
small private dining-room at the MacClelland Inn.
The three windows looked out over the side garden. We sat around a table. Vicky, Dr. Don Higel,
John Tennant and I were having coffee. Larry
Arma was having a Coke. Chief Perry Score was
having nothing. He sat at the head of the table.
There were eight chairs at the table. The one at the
foot of the table was empty, as was the one at the
right of Chief Score.

Nancy Paulson was in the adjoining room with
her mother. Her father was at home because after
Mr. Paulson had been informed of Mackin's act
seven years ago, Higel had had to keep him under
constant heavy sedation.

In the expectant silence Perry Score kept glar-
ing at me. It annoyed him that Quillan, after a

chat with Larry Arma, refused to sign a complaint against me.

Score said irritably, "I don't like this at all. It isn't legal procedure. It's a damn parlor game."

"Sometimes," Tennant said, "the ends of justice are better served by informal methods. We have an eighteen-year-old girl involved here. She is reacting remarkably well to all this. But what would a public scandal do to her? Would you care to take that chance?"

"This is all just a fancy way of saying you have absolutely no evidence against Billy Mackin," Score said. "It's a coincidence. The Landy boy killed the other Paulson girl."

Vicky spoke up, her voice cool. "There is not one other person at this table who believes that, sir."

Score retreated into a grumpy silence.

Larry Arma riffled the pages of his stenographic notebook, then glanced at his watch. "Think he'll show, John? He's ten minutes overdue."

"I hope he doesn't show," Tennant said. "I hope he runs like a rabbit. But if he does show, I want to repeat to you people what I said before. And you pay particular attention, Score. I'm going to do some lying. Back me up. Play it by ear."

Charlie Staubs opened the door and stuck his head in. "He's coming," he said.

"Send him in," Tennant said.

Billy Mackin came into the room thirty seconds later. He paused inside the door, smiling, hat in his hand. His glance took in all of us, and the smile did not slip.

"Sorry I'm a little late," he said. "Very mysterious summons. What's it all about?" As he spoke he took off his topcoat, hung coat and hat on the tree, and headed for the chair next to Score.

"Please sit at the end of the table, Mr. Mackin," Tennant said. "You are intelligent enough, I know, to make a good guess as to what this is all about. I'm sure you know everybody here, and you know what we all have in common."

Mackin sat down, took out his cigarettes. "The Landy case, I suppose. I don't know why I should be here."

"That's what we want to explain to you."

Mackin looked disapprovingly at Arma. "This man is taking notes. Is there something official about this? Is this some kind of a hearing?"

"This is entirely informal. It has no official cachet. You are free to leave at any time, Mr. Mackin. But a record will be kept. Should you wish to leave, I am certain you will have the opportunity of speaking up at a more official hearing."

"Are you threatening me, Mr. Tennant?"

"No. We have come into the possession of certain facts. If you can make a satisfactory explanation of those facts, it will save all the risk and embarrassment and publicity of a false arrest. Is that fair?"

"I—I suppose so," he said.

Tennant slowly turned the pages of a small brown notebook. "We have sworn statements from two minors that Jane Ann Paulson received money from you in odd amounts on no set schedule, but that over a period of time, it added up to a considerable sum. We have a record of many expensive purchases she made, and her father's statement that she received no allowance. Can you explain that?"

Mackin smiled and said with assurance, "I certainly can. Jane Ann was a wild kid, but she was a good kid. I guess you know, all of you, that I'm very close to the Paulsons. I'm like an uncle to those two girls. Dick was too hard on Jane Ann. A girl likes pretty things. She likes a little fun. I helped her out when she needed money. I can't see any harm in that."

Tennant turned another page. "In February of this year you defaulted on a note and it was renewed. It was rather a small note. Many weeks after Jane Ann was murdered over eight hundred dollars was found in her room. Do you not think you were over-generous?"

"Eight hundred dollars!" he cried. "What do you think I am? I'd slip her a five, sometimes a ten. If she was getting that kind of money, she was getting it from somebody else. I guess you know about the time she stayed in that fraternity house. There's some pretty well-to-do kids up on the hill. Maybe she was peddling. Maybe she stole it. I didn't give her that kind of money."

I was forced to respect the quickness of his mind and the plausibility of his manner. He had covered himself by making a minor admission. It began to seem incredible to me that this man could be what we thought him to be.

Score said warmly, "Bill, these people seem to—"

"I am conducting this," Tennant said sharply.

Score shrugged. "Go ahead. Have fun."

I looked at Mackin. Score's interruption seemed to give him strength.

Tennant turned more pages. "You claim that you were working at your store on the night of the crime. The lights were on in your back office, as well as the night light in the store proper. You were seen leaving the rear of the store early in the evening."

Mackin banged the flat of his hand on the table top. "Now just a moment! I can see where you're heading. This is utterly ridiculous. I do not have to sit here and be accused of anything."

Tennant looked at him mildly. "Then leave."

Mackin eyed the notebook. He seemed as though ready to leave, then settled down again. "I'll help all I can. But I go on record as saying this is absurd."

"You're on record," Arma said quietly.

"It's hard to remember that far back. Maybe I did leave the store and return. I keep some of my records at home. Sometimes I find I need some records from the house. So I leave and get them and come back. It happens often. I may have left that night to do that or to go get some coffee. I really couldn't remember. Does it matter?"

"Some of your records are kept on three by five file cards, are they not?"

Mackin looked at Tennant with perfect blankness. "Eh? Yes. The charge account file. Some of the inventory records."

"Unruled cards?"

"I don't get it. Yes."

"You stock several brands of glue and paste don't you?"

"Certainly."

"Would you be willing to turn over blank samples of your card file stock and samples of the glue and paste you stock for laboratory analysis?"

Mackin shook his head in a bewildered way. "This I don't get. Sure. I'd do that, but I don't see what it could mean."

Score shifted restlessly. Tennant let the silence grow. He nodded. He put the notebook down, and said, "In all fairness to you, Mackin, I want you to be *very* careful of your answer to this next question. Before you came to Dalton, were you ever in trouble with the law?"

The phrasing of the question was clever. If Tennant had no information it would be safe to say "no" quickly; or if he had been in no trouble, the "no" would be automatic. But if he had, he could assume from Tennant's warning that Tennant knew about it. And after three taut seconds had passed, Mackin realized he had waited too long. I saw a first gleam of sweat on his upper lip.

"It was one of those things," he said. "I got caught in a box. A town in Indiana. I looked too crummy to get a hitch. I was hitting the farms, trying to work for a handout and get a chance to clean up. This woman got pretty friendly. I guess you know what I mean. Then she must have looked out the window and seen her old man coming in from the field. She started screaming and carrying on and she tore her own clothes. I ran for it. They picked me up in the next town. I was booked for rape, but they didn't want to fuss and after ten days they gave me a release to sign, they drove me over the state line and beat hell out of me. Any kid could have gotten caught in the same box."

Tennant was making the most effective use of silences. Mackin lighted another cigarette. His hands shook slightly.

"Nothing else?" Tennant asked.

"No," Mackin said too quickly.

"You're positive of that?"

Mackin shrugged. "You bum around, you get booked for vagrancy. California is tough. I'm not counting those times."

"Wasn't there something more than vagrancy? Certainly you can remember."

Mackin's face darkened. "Nothing else. Nothing." But I think that even Score sensed he was lying. Score's expression had changed. He was looking at Mackin warily and he seemed puzzled.

Tennant nodded at Vicky. She got up and went to the other door. I did not turn to watch Nancy come in. I watched Mackin. For just a moment his eyes narrowed and his mouth tautened, and then his expression was normal again. Nancy sat at Score's right, between him and Tennant.

Tennant said, "My dear, I know this is going to be very unpleasant for you. But, believe me, if I can help it, nothing you say will go further than this room. Tell us what happened to you on that Labor Day week end when you were eleven."

Nancy moistened her lips. Her face was chalky. She did not look toward Mackin. She kept her face turned away. She told the story in a small emotionless voice, in short sentences, with little descriptive detail. But it was a powerful and frightening story.

"Can you remember how Mr. Mackin was dressed?"

"Yes. He had been working on the roof. He had on tan pants. He didn't have a shirt on. He was sweaty. His eyes were funny."

"What do you remember afterwards?"

"I was just walking. I didn't know where I was going. My throat hurt. I carried my dress for a long time and I remember I stopped and put it on."

"You are certain now that it was Billy Mackin?"

She turned her head very slowly and she looked at him with dead eyes, eyes too old for her face. "It was Uncle Billy."

At a nod from Tennant, Vicky went around the table and got her and took her back to her mother. She resumed her seat. We all looked at Mackin. He seemed on the verge of speaking several times. He slumped lower in the chair. His face had become masklike.

"She's mistaken," he said.

"Do you really think so?" Tennant asked gently.

"I—I get a little out of control. I mean I used to. I've outgrown it. I fought it. I'm all right now. Have been for years. I didn't do anything to her."

"Except nearly scaring her out of her mind."

"I heard somebody coming. I didn't do anything." He mumbled the words. I could barely hear him.

I knew we had enough to drive him out of the town, to collapse the personality he had built up. But not enough to save Alister. I knew that there had to be some hard blow that would shatter the whole structure.

"You didn't do anything," Tennant said. "You still wanted her. You waited a long time. Nobody else was going to have her. Now it's all ruined for you, isn't it?"

Mackin seemed to realize how much damage had been done him. He looked alarmed. He straightened up and the plausible smile was back. "You can't condemn a man for a mistake a long time ago. I'm respected in this town. I've got good friends here."

Score spoke up. "You *were* respected. You *had* friends."

"You won't be able to stay here, Mackin," Tennant said, "You'll be back on the road again. It's all gone now."

"You people can't do that to me!"

"We won't. The town will," Higel said.

I imagine that Tennant had been waiting for Mackin to become highly agitated. In a sharp voice he said, "And why were you stupid enough to pick Jane Ann up under a street light?"

"It was dark where—" And in a gesture like that of a child, he clamped his right hand over his mouth. His eyes stared at us over the tense hand. His eyes closed and his hand dropped into his lap. His head sagged. I could see his chest lift and fall with his breathing. There was silence in the room. Tears ran down Vicky's cheeks. Score looked as though somebody had hit him in the belly. Arma was cool, professional, remote. Tennant merely looked weary. He closed the notebook and put it back in his pocket.

"All right," Mackin said without opening his eyes. "All right." His voice was subdued, resigned.

"From the beginning," Tennant said.

"All right. I heard them talking. Nancy and the Howard kid. Robby Howard. I heard them talking about running away. Jane Ann was being punished. Dick had locked her in the top of the boathouse. I didn't know that. There was a little window in front. She could see the dock. I sat on the edge of the dock. He came swimming."

Tennant and I exchanged puzzled glances.

"I pushed him under with my feet. He was a strong kid. He should have swum away. He kept coming back. I kept pushing him under. He tried to grab my ankles. Then he didn't try any more. I saw him for a while under the water and then I couldn't see him any more. I didn't know she saw it. She kept hanging around me. I didn't know what she had on her mind. It wasn't until Christmas that year that it started. She told me; and I gave her money to keep her quiet. She kept asking for more. She didn't have any proof. But it would have made trouble. I shouldn't have given her money. That made it look bad if she told later. I took it out of the register each time."

He shielded his eyes with his hand. It was several moments before he resumed. He explained how carefully he had planned it, how many false starts he had made, and how the timing had finally worked out.

When he started to tell of the actual killing, Vicky got up and left the room. I followed her out, closing the door behind me, shutting out the drone of the tired, defeated voice. I caught her and held her in my arms. She was trembling.

There isn't much more. When Alister was released, he had to be institutionalized. We were told that the prognosis was favorable, and that a complete recovery could be expected in a few months. They said it would be better to permit no visitors. And the man in charge of the case, a Dr. Dougherty, was severe with Vicky for having overprotected Alister. He told her to live her own life.

We found a place for a honeymoon. Down in Pine Island Sound below Boca Grande, a place called Cabbage Key, run by nice people. There she relearned the knack of gaiety, but there is still a cloud over my bride. It dwindles month by month; but there will be, for all her life, that streak of darkness, that stain left upon her by disaster.

After my marriage my employers began to look more kindly upon me. Vicky made a good impression on the staff. They gave me my own job to run, a piece of a turnpike in North Carolina.

Now it is April, and that black week is six months ago, and Mackin still awaits execution. His wife died five months ago. Alister visited with us a week before going up to Philadelphia where he will do graduate work. There is no arrogance left in him. He is, perhaps, too silent. He told us about Nancy. They plan to be married in the summer. It can be either a very good marriage or a very bad one. It is up to the two of them.

It is April and spring comes early in the Carolinas. We have rented this dim little house full of borax furniture. Vicky does not seem to mind that we will live like nomads for many years. It is Saturday afternoon and I have come home from the dusty job and showered. From the bedroom window I can see her out in the small back yard. She is sitting on her heels, earnestly grubbing in what may turn out to be a flower bed. The trowel is red and her sunsuit is yellow and her back is tanned by spring sun. She looks very intent and very delectable. Her little bottom is trim and handsome in yellow linen. I feel a pleasant sense of possession, of responsibility. I feel extraordinarily lucky.

"Hey!" I say through the screen.

She tilts her head and squints up at me. "Hey to you."

"Come on up here a minute."

"What for?"

I growl. I consider it quite a respectable effort. She gives a large and knowing sigh, burlesques great reluctance, discards garden trowel and trudges toward the back door. Seven seconds later she is in my arms.

ABOUT THE AUTHOR

John D. MacDonald was graduated from Syracuse University and received an MBA from the Harvard Business School. He and his wife Dorothy, had one son and several grandchildren. Mr. MacDonald died in December 1986.